Harry Castlemon

Frank Nelson in the Forecastle

The Sportsman's Club Among the Whalers

Harry Castlemon

Frank Nelson in the Forecastle
The Sportsman's Club Among the Whalers

ISBN/EAN: 9783337327774

Printed in Europe, USA, Canada, Australia, Japan

Cover: Foto ©Andreas Hilbeck / pixelio.de

More available books at **www.hansebooks.com**

FRANK NELSON

IN THE FORECASTLE;

OR, THE

SPORTSMAN'S CLUB AMONG THE WHALERS.

By HARRY CASTLEMON, ·

AUTHOR OF "THE SPORTSMAN'S CLUB SERIES," "GUNBOAT SERIES," "ROLLING STONE SERIES," &C.

PHILADELPHIA:

PORTER & COATES.

CINCINNATI:

R. W. CARROLL & CO.

FAMOUS CASTLEMON BOOKS.

GUNBOAT SERIES. By HARRY CASTLEMON. Illustrated. 6 vols. 16mo. Cloth, extra, black and gold.

FRANK THE YOUNG NATURALIST. FRANK ON A GUNBOAT. FRANK IN THE WOODS. FRANK BEFORE VICKSBURG. FRANK ON THE LOWER MISSISSIPPI. FRANK ON THE PRAIRIE.

ROCKY MOUNTAIN SERIES. By HARRY CASTLEMON. Illustrated. 3 vols. 16mo. Cloth, extra, black and gold.

FRANK AMONG THE RANCHEROS.

FRANK AT DON CARLOS' RANCHO.

FRANK IN THE MOUNTAINS.

SPORTSMAN'S CLUB SERIES. By HARRY CASTLEMON. Illustrated. 3 vols. 16mo. Cloth, extra, black and gold.

THE SPORTSMAN'S CLUB IN THE SADDLE.

THE SPORTSMAN'S CLUB AFLOAT.

THE SPORTSMAN'S CLUB AMONG THE TRAPPERS.

GO-AHEAD SERIES. By HARRY CASTLEMON. Illustrated. 3 vols. 16mo. Cloth, extra, black and gold.

TOM NEWCOMBE. GO-AHEAD. NO MOSS.

FRANK NELSON SERIES. By HARRY CASTLEMON. Illustrated. 3 vols. 16mo. Cloth, extra, black and gold.

SNOWED UP. FRANK IN THE FORECASTLE. BOY TRADERS.

BOY TRAPPER SERIES. By HARRY CASTLEMON. Illustrated. 3 vols. 16mo. Cloth, extra, black and gold.

THE BURIED TREASURE; OR, OLD JORDAN'S HAUNT.

THE BOY TRAPPER; OR, HOW DAVE FILLED THE ORDER.

THE MAIL-CARRIER.

ROUGHING IT SERIES. By HARRY CASTLEMON. Illustrated. 16mo. Cloth, extra, black and gold.

GEORGE IN CAMP.

Other Volumes in Preparation.

Entered according to Act of Congress, in the year 1876 by
R. W. CARROLL & CO.,
In the Office of the Librarian of Congress, at Washington.

CONTENTS.

CONTENTS.

FRANK NELSON
IN THE FORECASTLE;

OR, THE

SPORTSMAN'S CLUB AMONG THE WHALERS.

CHAPTER I.

A BACKWOODSMAN'S IDEAS.

I DECLARE this is almost like coming into another world, isn't it?"

"Yes, and I, for one, am glad to get back. I like a good horse, and no one enjoys a few days' shooting and fishing better than I do ; but when I get tired of the saddle and the woods, I like to see the blue water and feel the solid planks of a yacht's deck under my feet once more. We had a good time though, in spite of all our adventures and mishaps."

"We certainly did. I am like Perk, who, after he had been down into the Cave of the Winds, under Niagara Falls, said he would do it again for no money, but seeing that he *had* been down, he would not sell his experience at any price. I couldn't be hired to make that same trip to Fort Bolton again— being "snowed up" was the worst part of it to me— but since it is all over and we are safely out of it, I am glad we went."

This was a portion of the conversation carried on by our friends Archie, Fred and Eugene, as they sat in the main-crosstrees of the Stranger, swinging their feet in the air and looking out over the shipping anchored off North Point Dock, in the harbor of San Francisco. They had only just arrived that day, their trip across the mountains being happily ended. They had discarded the half-savage, half-civilized costumes they had worn during their sojourn in the wilderness and substituted pea-jackets for their hunting-shirts, light shoes for their high-top boots, and natty tarpaulins for their slouch hats. They looked as though they had just come out of some lady's band-box, and one and all declared that it was most refreshing to find themselves dressed up like white folks once more.

The first thing these three uneasy youngsters did after they had donned their "shore clothes," and put the suits they had worn in the mountains carefully away in their trunks for safe-keeping, was to run all over the vessel, looking into every locker and corner, just as they had done when they first saw her on the stocks at New Orleans, and the next to mount to the crosstrees to survey the harbor. Here they had sat for half an hour, enjoying the prospect spread out before them, and talking over their recent adventures and exploits. The other members of the Club, Walter, Frank Nelson, George Le Dell and the rest, were seated on the quarter-deck with Uncle Dick, talking to Dick Lewis and old Bob Kelly.

Dick and Bob were objects of great interest to the sailors who composed the Stranger's crew. They stared at everything with wide-open eyes, and were as much out of place on the schooner's deck as the jolly tars would have been in the mountains from which the backwoodsmen had just arrived.

The Club had had a varied and eventful experience during the comparatively short time that they had been absent from the Stranger, and even now the hearts of some of them would beat a trifle faster whenever they thought of what they had passed through. Walter drew a long breath every time he recalled his experience in Potter's rancho; Fred and Eugene shivered and drew their collars up around their ears when they thought of the sight presented to their gaze on the day they set out from their camp under the cliffs, to show the Pike and his family the way to Fort Bolton, and imagined that they could see the air filled with driving snow, and could hear the roaring of the wind as it swept the prairie, just as they had seen it and heard it on that long-to-be-remembered afternoon. Archie grew excited and elated whenever he thought of the way he had captured the wild horse, and then exasperated when he remembered how he had lost him before he had had a chance to try even one race with his cousin. Frank shrugged his shoulders when any of his companions called him "Chinny Billy," as they often did, and thanked his lucky stars that he was well out of the predicament which the genuine Chinny Billy had so nearly got him into, when he denounced him as an impostor and spy in the presence of all the members of Potter's gang; and even Uncle Dick Gaylord, hardened as he was by a long life of adventure, did not like to recall the feelings of anxiety and suspense that he had experienced on more than one occasion, during the journey to Bolton and back. The two trappers were probably the only ones in the party for whom the last few months had no especial interest. Their lives were made up of just such scenes and incidents, and they never thought of them again, unless something happened to bring them vividly to their recollection.

The last night that the friends passed at Fort Bolton was given up to enjoyment. The colonel and major entertained Uncle Dick at their quarters, and the younger officers took charge of the boys.

After supper it was noticed that some of the officers
and their guests distributed themselves in little
groups about the room, that the members of each
group carried on a very earnest conversation in a
low tone of voice, and that various little keepsakes
were passed from one to the other, which each
promised to preserve in remembrance of the giver.
The gifts that passed between Frank and Lieutenant
Gaylord were the most valuable of any. These two
young fellows had been fast friends and almost
constant companions ever since the night on which
the lieutenant recaptured Dick Lewis after his
flight from the guard house, and arrested Frank for
assisting him to make his escape. Frank had something he knew the lieutenant wanted, and that was
the splendid horse which Potter had given him.
Frank could not take the animal around the world
with him, and besides he was already the happy
owner of a steed which was just as handsome and
swift, and which held a much higher place in his
affections. That was Roderick. It was Uncle
Dick's intention to travel on horseback until the

party reached a point from which they could continue their journey by stage or railroad, and then sell off their stock—their wagon, which would have been an almost useless encumbrance to them, now that the roads were blocked with snow, having been exchanged for pack mules—Frank would then have no further use for his horse, so he offered him to the lieutenant, who was glad to accept him.

The journey to San Francisco was made without the occurrence of any exciting or noteworthy incidents. Among them all they managed to shoot a few black-tails, and one grizzly bear, whose skin and claws were preserved by the old members of the Club as trophies. They found the snow fully as deep as they expected, the travelling difficult, and the weather extremely cold; but their progress was steady, although slow, until they reached the railroad, and then in a few hours they found themselves in an almost tropical climate.

When they reached the railroad, Dick and Old Bob would have taken leave of them, but the boys would not listen to it. They were determined that,

if they could have their own way, the trappers
should remain with them for a long time to come.
They owed much to these two men, and as they
could not repay them in any other way, they would
take them around the world, introducing them to
scenes and people of which they had never dreamed.
Of course this idea originated with rattle-brained
Eugene Gaylord, and Uncle Dick, who could not
find it in his heart to refuse his nephews anything
they asked for, consented to the arrangement,
though not without a good deal of grumbling.

"They'll only be in the way, Eugene," said the
old sailor. "They just fit the mountains and the
prairie—they were made for them; but how will
they look on the deck of the Stranger? There
isn't room enough aboard our little craft for that
giant, Louis."

"O, Uncle, there are two or three empty bunks
in the forecastle, and they can sleep there as well
as not," replied Eugene.

"But they will be so uneasy that they'll not
enjoy themselves in the least," continued Uncle

Dick. " They will be frightened to death when they find themselves out of sight of land, and the men will be playing tricks on them all the while."

" But the men mustn't play tricks on them. We won't let them ; and besides it would be dangerous. As for being out of sight of land, that need not trouble them. They'll not be in half as much danger as they were while they were with Potter's gang. Then think of the fun we'll have, Uncle! Didn't you notice how they opened their eyes the other night when Bab was telling them of the elephants we expect to see in India ?"

" Well, well! do as you please," said the old sailor. " If they are foolish enough to go, I shall have a fine time of it among you all; I can see that plainly." And then he turned away to hunt up Frank Nelson, to whom he always went when he had anything on his mind.

Eugene having gained his point went straight to Archie and Fred, who declared that it was the best thing they ever heard of. The matter was laid before the trappers with as little delay as possible, and the proposition almost took their breath away. They opened their mouths and eyes and looked wonderingly at each other, but said nothing. Archie thought that was enough for one day, and although his friends wanted an immediate answer, he succeeded in inducing them to retire and leave the trappers to themselves. He thought it best to give them leisure to turn the matter over in their minds (it seemed to be more than they could grasp at once) and go to them for an answer at some future time.

Dick and old Bob seemed to grow timid as they approached the confines of civilization, but they were coaxed on board the train, and when the party reached San Francisco, they were taken off to the Stranger. The matter of the voyage around the world had been brought for up discussion a few times, but Dick had found his tongue at last, and declared that it was not to be thought of. The boys knew better than to press the subject, and hoped that time would accomplish what arguments could never do. A few hours on board the Stranger in the harbor, where vessels were constantly coming and going, might increase their confidence, while it familiarized them in some slight degree with life on ship-board, and perhaps they could then be induced to change their minds. Archie had tried to persuade Dick to follow him and his companions to the cross-trees; but the trapper, after glancing down at his colossal proportions, and then up at the ratlines, which looked no larger than so many threads, declared that the ropes wouldn't bear his weight, and remained below.

"Now, this feels natural!" exclaimed Feather-weight, swinging back and forth on his dizzy perch with such apparent recklessness that Dick Lewis, who now and then looked up at him, fairly shook in his moccasins; "and I am ready for new adventures and new sights beyond the seas. Our fellows can say, what the books tell us comparatively few American travellers can say, and that is, we have seen the most of the wonders of our own country. I never expect to see anything grander than the

Yo Semite Valley. I wonder how long it will be before Uncle Dick will hoist the signal for sailing?"

"Just as soon as the stores are aboard," said Eugene. "We may get off to-morrow."

"Will Dick and Bob go with us?"

"No," said Archie. "We might as well give that up. And since I have come to think of it, I don't want them to go unless they are perfectly willing to do so."

"Nor I," said Eugene. "If it frightens them so badly to travel on a railroad train, what would be their feelings when they found the schooner tossing about on such waves as we saw coming around the Horn? I shall urge them no more."

"They have been talking to Frank about it," continued Fred. "They always go to him and believe every word he says—that is, almost every word."

"Ah! yes; I was going to put that in," said Archie. "They don't like to believe that the world is round. They don't say so with their mouths, but they do with their eyes."

"And they don't know what to think about elephants as large as that house of Potter's, and lions and tigers, and snakes twenty feet long," said Fred.

"And a whale bothers them," chimed in Eugene; "and Dick laughed the other day when I told him about a flying-fish."

"What's going on down there?" asked Archie, as the sound of voices in animated conversation came up from the deck.

The boys looked below and saw that the group, which they had last seen scattered over the quarter-deck, were gathered about Dick Lewis, who appeared to be making them a speech. Now and then he illustrated his remarks by pointing to something he had placed at his feet; but the boys could not see what it was, for the Club were crowded about it and hid it from view. They were missing something, that was evident; but they did not intend to miss any more of it, and it was but the work of a few seconds to swing themselves out of the crosstrees on to the ratlines, and descend to the deck. They

2

ran up to the group, and found that the object over which the trapper was holding forth was simply a mess-pan filled with water.

"Them stories you've been a tellin' seems wonderful to me an' ole Bob, who never heard the like afore," Dick was saying as the boys came up. "We don't conspute 'em, 'cause bein' unedicated men, we never had no book larnin', an' don't know nothing outside the mountains an' the prairy. Now, you tell me that thar's three times as much water on the 'arth as thar is ground; that you're goin' to start from Fr'isco an' sail clean around it in this yere little boat, an' that if me an' ole Bob'll go with you, we won't even know that we're sailing round the world. Won't we know when we come to the edge?"

"There isn't any edge to it," said Frank.

"Sho! Thar can't help bein' an edge if the world is round, can thar? This yere," said Dick, pointing to the pan of water, "is the sea; an' this yere," he continued, fumbling in the pockets of his hunting shirt, "is the 'arth."

As he spoke he drew out a piece of hard tack, which he had rudely shaped with his knife to represent his idea of the rotundity of the earth. The corners were cut off, making the biscuit nearly round, and there was a piece clipped out of the side of it, in shape something like a bottle with a very short neck and wide body, to represent the Golden Gate and the harbor of San Francisco. This miniature world Dick placed in the middle of the pan of water, and then straightened up and looked triumphantly at his audience. Eugene glanced at it, choked back a laugh and then rushed off to find the steward, while the trapper went on with his illustration.

"Now, thar's the 'arth," said he, placing his finger on the biscuit, "flat like a pan-cake, as anybody can see it is, that's ever been out on the prairie, an' round like *you* say it is. Here is the sea all around it, an' here's Fr'isco. Now, after you go out of the Golden Gate an' start to sail round the 'arth," said Dick, moving his long finger through the water around the biscuit, "can't you see the edge all the way round? I can understand that, which wasn't so very plain to me a few days ago, but now comes something I can't see into. You say the 'arth turns over onct every day, but that don't by no means stand to reason, 'cause jest see what would happen,"—he went on, placing his finger under the biscuit and raising one edge of it out of the water. "If it turned over, one side of it would keep gettin' higher an' higher all the time, an' finally the houses, an' trees, an' mountains, an' folks would get to slidin' an' slidin', an' when they come to the edge, they'd all slip off into the water; an' when the 'arth turned *cl'ar* over"—here he flopped the biscuit up side down in the pan—"whar would we all be?"

None of his auditors had attempted to interrupt the trapper, and the reason was because there was not one among them who could trust himself to speak, not even Uncle Dick. Believing from their silence that he had got the better of all of them, the trapper said he was more firmly convinced than he had ever been before, that all the learning in the

world was not to be found in books, and was about
to throw the contents of his mess-pan over the side,
when Eugene came elbowing his way into the group,
carrying an apple in on hand and a small magnet in
the other.

"Now, Dick," said he, "let me talk a minute.
You haven't quite got the idea. In the first place,
that piece of hard tack doesn't represent the shape
of the earth, but this-apple does, pretty nearly.
In the next place, the globe doesn't revolve through
water, for the water forms part of the earth and
turns with it."

"Sho!" exclaimed the trapper. "It would all
spill out."

"Hold on a minute, and I'll show you that it
can't spill out. The world revolves through the
air. Don't you fellows criticise now," continued
Eugene, turning to his companions. "If, when I
get through, you·want to explain that the earth
really revolves through space, and that the air goes
with it, except such portions as are left behind and

form the trade-winds, you are welcome to do it; but it is quite beyond me."

Eugene handed the magnet to Archie to hold until he was ready to use it, and with the point of his knife rudely traced upon the apple the shape of the continents and the principal oceans. This done, he went on with his explanation, which was simply a repetition of what every boy learns when he first begins the study of geography. He described the motions of the earth as well as he could, and used the magnet to illustrate the attraction of gravitation. Dick listened attentively, and when Eugene finished, took the apple from his hand and looked at it with a great deal of interest. He turned it over several times, and appeared to be meditating upon something.

" They're goin' to sail round the 'arth this way," said he, moving his finger slowly around the circumference of the apple, and talking more to himself than to the boys standing about, "an' when they get around here"—he stopped and thought a moment, holding the end of his finger under the

apple—'' when they get around here, they'll be—
Human natur'!'' he cried suddenly, as if frightened
at the discovery he had made. "When you get
around here, on the under side of the 'arth, you'll
be walkin' with your heads downwards, won't you?
Bob can do as he likes, but *I* won't go. Mebbe
that little red hoss-shoe aint strong enough to hold
the boat fast to the 'arth—don't look as if it was—
an' some dark night she'll get to fallin' an' fallin'—
Whew! I'm as near that place now as I want to be,
an' I'm off fur the mountains to-morrow, bright an'
'arly.''

Dick turned away, fairly trembling with excitement, and the boys scattered as if some one had
suddenly sent a charge of bird-shot among them.

CHAPTER II.

"MAN OVERBOARD."

THE trappers were badly frightened, there could be no doubt about that, and it was a spectacle the Club had never expected to witness. That these two men, who had time and again faced death in almost every shape in which he presents himself on shore, who had lived in the very midst of danger from their youth up, and who sought and delighted in perilous exploits, should be so nearly overcome with terror by hearing of things with which every schoolboy is familiar, was surprising; and there was something so ludicrous in the manner in which they exhibited their alarm, that the boys could scarcely restrain their laughter until they could get out of sight. Old Bob glared wildly about him, seemingly on the point of jumping overboard and swimming ashore, and Dick Lewis leaned against the rail, drawing his breath in quick gasps and looking altogether as if he did not yet fairly understand the startling discovery he had made. Uncle Dick Gaylord took one glance at him and then went to the stern and looked over into the water, while the boys dived down into the cabin and threw themselves into chairs, or leaned up in corners, holding their handkerchiefs over their mouths—all except Archie, who never could control himself when he wanted to laugh. He ran into his state-room, shut the door and buried his head in the pillows. The funny part of it was, that Dick should suppose that those who attempted the reckless task of sailing around the world, should be obliged to take a magnet with them, in order to keep themselves and their vessel from falling off when they reached the "under side of the earth."

At the end of five minutes Archie made an attempt to come out into the cabin, but he was still bubbling over with laughter, and the sight of him created a fresh explosion, and set Archie himself to going again at such a rate that he was obliged to go back. It is hard to tell how long it would have been before the boys could have controlled themselves sufficiently to talk the matter over, had it not been that a commotion which suddenly arose on deck, drew their attention to other affairs.

"Fore rigging, there," exclaimed Uncle Dick. "What do you see?"

"A man overboard, sir," replied the voice of the boatswain's mate. "He jumped off that whaler, sir."

"And he's swimming this way, sir," said another voice, "and making signals of distress."

"Have the cutter called away, Mr. Baldwin," said Uncle Dick, to his first mate, "and send a crew out to pick him up."

The boys waited to hear no more. They crowded up the companion ladder with such haste that they ran some risk of sticking fast in the narrow passageway, and reached the deck just as the crew of the cutter were tumbling into their boat which lay along side moored to a swinging boom, man-of-war fashion.

"Where is Mr. Parker?" said Uncle Dick, looking around for his second officer.

"O, let me go in charge of the boat, Uncle," exclaimed Eugene, snatching Fred's hat from his head, for he had left his own in the cabin.

"Away you go, then," said the old sailor. "Don't let him sink before you reach him."

"They're sending out a boat from the whaler, sir," said the foremast hand, who was at work in the forward rigging, and who had been the first to discover the man in the water.

"Does he appear to be all right?"

"O, yes, sir. He swims like a duck, but he's waving his hand to us."

"Hold on a minute, Eugene."

Uncle Dick sprang upon the rail and supporting himself by the shrouds looked towards the man, and then toward the boat that was coming out to pick him up, while the boys, all except Eugene, who stood ready to take his place in the cutter at a moment's warning, swarmed up the rigging and looked on with no little interest. They saw at once that the man had no trouble in keeping afloat, for he swam over the waves as buoyantly as a cork. They saw, too, that he did not want to be overtaken by the whaler's boat, if he could help it, for he looked back at her occasionally to see if she was gaining on him, and then redoubled his efforts to reach the schooner.

"He is trying to desert," said Uncle Dick, "and I think we had better have nothing to do with him."

"Quartermaster, pass up that spy-glass," said Frank.

The petty officer handed the instrument to Featherweight, who happened to be lowest in the shrouds, and he passed it to George Le Dell, who handed it up to Frank. The latter mounted to the crosstrees and levelled the glass at the swimmer. He held it to his eye for a few minutes, and then passing it back to George, said :

"That man has either met with a severe accident, or been roughly handled. His face is bleeding."

"Help! help!" cried a faint voice.

". Go and pick him up," said Uncle Dick.

" Shove off," commanded Eugene, before he was fairly seated in the stern-sheets of the cutter. " Remember, men, that you are racing with a whale-boat, and that you don't want to be beaten."

The cutter swung around with her bow toward the swimmer, and propelled by eight strong oars-men, who seemed to lift her fairly out of the water at every stroke, flew over the waves like a duck. A boat race was something in which Eugene took especial delight, but the one that came off that morning between the cutter and the whale-boat was not as exciting or as closely contested as he had hoped it would be. In fact it was no race at all; for when the officer, whoever he was, who had charge of the deck of the whaler, saw that the cutter was likely to reach the swimmer first, he hailed his boat, which turned around and went back.

" In bow," commanded the coxswain of the cutter, who was sitting just behind Eugene.

The two sailors who were seated in the bow raised their oars from the water, placed them on the thwarts between them, and then one stood up with the boat-hook in his hand, while the other threw himself flat on his face and extended his arm out over the water.

" Way enough !· Toss, and stand by," said the coxswain.

The other oars were all thrown up into the air at the same moment, laid upon the thwarts, and every man leaned over the side to be ready to seize the swimmer as the cutter moved past him. She retained steerage-way enough to carry her within a few feet of him, and then the coxswain, with one movement of the tiller, turned the bow aside, and the boat-hook was thrust out within reach of his hands. It was a matter of some difficulty to haul the rescued man aboard, for he was too nearly exhausted to help himself, and his clothing, being thoroughly saturated with water, was as heavy as so much lead. Besides, his forehead was badly cut and bruised, and no doubt he was suffering from the hurt.

" Did you fall overboard ?" asked Eugene, after

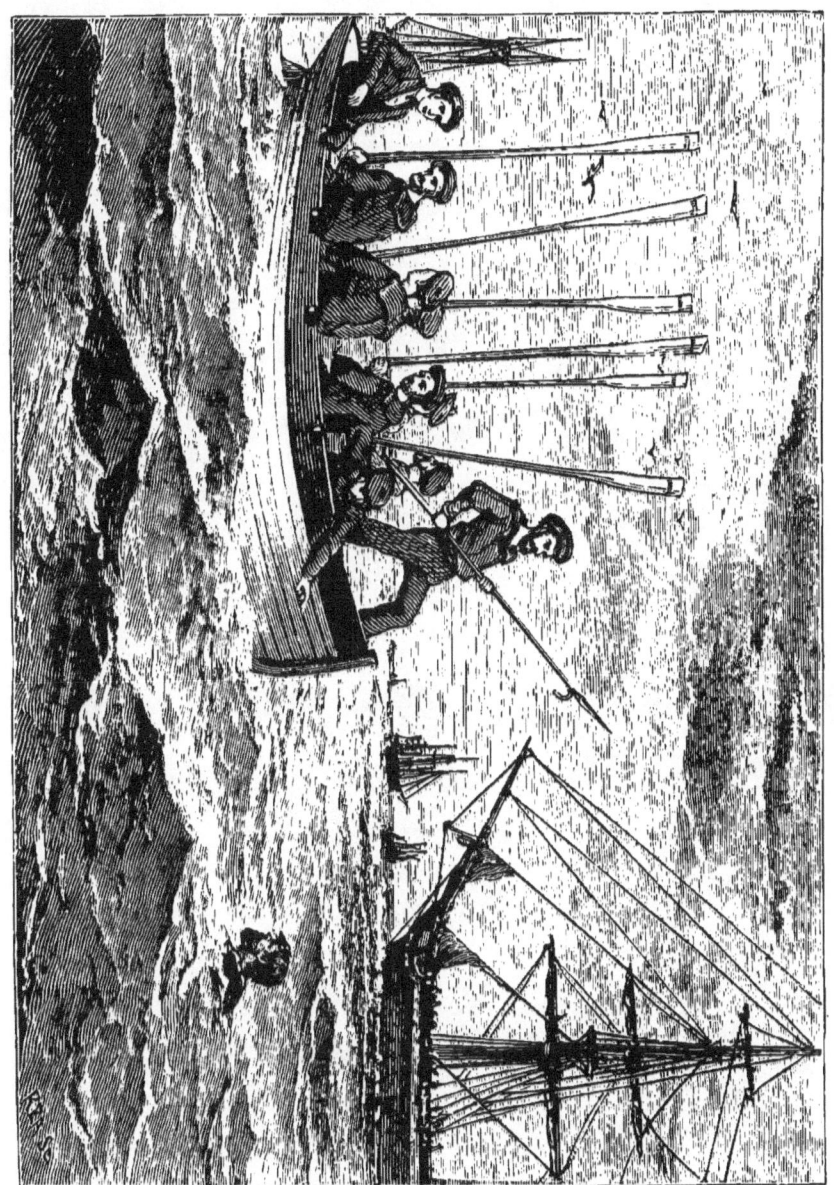

RESCUING THE DESERTER.

the man had been pulled into the boat and had taken his seat in the bow.

"No, sir; I jumped overboard on purpose."

"You hit your head against something, didn't you?"

"The cap'n hit it for me, sir. It was a belaying pin that made that mark."

Eugene looked wonderingly at the coxswain, who nodded his head, as if to say that he didn't doubt it at all.

"Why, the officers aboard our vessel don't find it necessary to do such things," said Eugene.

"But all vessels ain't like the Stranger, sir, nor are all shipmasters like Cap'n Gaylord," said the coxswain. "Do you s'pose there's a sailorman aboard of us that would do what this chap has done—try to desert? No, sir, you couldn't kick 'em off if you wanted to. When we get back to Bellville we'll have every man we brought away with us, unless some of 'em are in Davy's locker."

The cutter was soon alongside the schooner, and the rescued man, by dint of hauling from above and pushing from below, was got upon the deck. He was a pitiable object when one came to look at him, and Uncle Dick's first order was: "Take him below, some of you, and give him something fit to put on. Be in a hurry about it."

The sailors were only too glad to obey. They led the dripping man into the forecastle, from which he emerged a few minutes later with a clean face, a suit of dry clothes, and a handkerchief bound about his forehead. In his appearance, which was very much improved, he would have compared favorably with any of the seamen on board the Stranger, and they were the very best that Uncle Dick could find in the port of New Orleans. He had evidently had plenty of time to tell at least a portion of his story, for the faces of the sailors were as black as so many thunder clouds.

The rescued man at once made his way aft, accompanied by the boatswain's mate, who, presuming for this once upon his captain's good-nature, and his own position as ranking petty officer on board the Stranger, took the liberty to go where he knew he had no right except he was in performance of his duties. The men saluted, removed their caps and waited for Uncle Dick to speak to them.

"Well, Lucas, what do you want here?" asked the old sailor.

"I ax your pardon, cap'n, for coming on the quarter-deck at this time without an invite," replied the boatswain's mate, "but I just wanted to say to you, sir, that this man is black and blue from his head to his feet, so he is."

"How did he get that way?" asked Uncle Dick, while the boys ranged themselves behind him so that they could hear all that passed, "and why is he trying to desert?"

The mate stepped back and moved his hand toward the rescued man, as if to say that he would tell his own story, and the latter said:

"I don't want to desert my ship, cap'n. I am an able seaman, know my duty and am ready to do it, if I can only have plenty to eat and am allowed a wink of sleep now and then. I am trying to get ashore for protection ag'in' them tyrants aboard the

3

Tycoon, and I hope you won't send me back to them, sir."

"Go on," said Uncle Dick. "What has happened aboard that ship?"

"She is nearly two years out of Nantucket, on a whaling course, sir," said the man, "and there isn't a foremast hand aboard of her that she brought out with her. They've all deserted. She has to get a new crew at every port, and when she can't get 'em honest, she kidnaps 'em, sir. I shipped aboard of her, along with a lot of others, at Callao. We've been out only four months, and two of the men jumped overboard rather than stand the hard treatment they received. On the first day out the officers began on us and never let up. They kept us at work till we were ready to drop, brought us out of bed at night and made us walk the deck, and if we fell asleep as we walked, they knocked us down with a handspike or belaying-pin. They starved us almost to death, and then, because my boat's crew were too weak to save a whale we made fast to, they put us all in irons and pounded us with ropes' ends till we were insensible."

This was only the introduction to the long story the man had to tell, and to which his auditors listened with breathless interest. According to his account, the Tycoon was a horrible place, and the cruelties that were practised by the officers upon the defenceless seamen, were shocking. The man certainly bore unmistakable evidence of brutal treatment, and added weight to his story by declaring that he was not only willing but anxious to meet his persecutors in a court of justice. Everybody who listened to him was indignant.

"The men on board that vessel have a remedy in their own hands—two of them, if they only knew it," said Frank. "Why didn't they demand an interview with the American consul at the first port at which they touched?"

"It wouldn't have done no good, sir," said the sailor. "The cap'n wouldn't never let 'em see him, sir."

"He couldn't help himself," returned Frank.

"The law compels him to allow his men to go ashore at every port at which the ship may touch to lay their complaints, if they have any, before our representative; or, if there is any good reason why the men cannot go ashore, the captain must bring the consul aboard to see them, if they demand it."

If there was anything in which Frank was particularly well posted, it was the law governing the duties of consuls, as some of our representatives in foreign countries are called. The attorney with whom he had been studying in Lawrence, had political aspirations, and had at one time expected to be appointed consul for some port in the Mediterranean. If he had succeeded in his object Frank would have gone with him as assistant and clerk. He did not wish to accept any situation with whose duties and responsibilities he was not familiar, and in order to fit himself for it, he had obtained a copy of the Consular Regulations, which he had thoroughly mastered. It is a part of the consul's duty to care for destitute, discharged and deserting seamen, to stand between foremast hands and tyrannical officers, to protect officers from and punish mutinous sailors, and Frank knew the law bearing upon every case that could possibly arise.

"The consul is obliged to listen to any and all complaints," continued Frank. "He measures them by the law bearing upon them, and he can discharge the crew on complaint of the officers, or he can discharge the officers themselves on a well-founded complaint from the crew."

The sailors opened their eyes and looked at one another. They had never dreamed that they had so many rights, or that there was a law enacted on purpose to protect them.

Just then the whale-boat came in sight again, rounding the stern of the Tycoon. She turned her bow toward the Stranger, and the quartermaster, after looking at her through his spy-glass, said there was a man in the stern-sheets dressed in gray. "That's the cap'n," exclaimed the deserter, in great alarm. "You won't let him take me back, sir?" he added, in a pleading voice.

"I can't prevent your lawful captain from taking you wherever he may find you," answered Uncle Dick; "but hold on, now, till I get through," he added, as the man began to back toward the rail as if he were about to take to the water again. "I'll give you a chance to save yourself. Call away the cutter, Mr. Baldwin, and send this man ashore."

"Thank you, cap'n, thank you," said the sailor gratefully, and with tears in his eyes. "A prosperous and pleasant voyage to you and your mates, sir. What shall I do when I get ashore, sir?" he continued, looking at Frank.

"Go to the nearest justice and take out a warrant against those officers for assault and battery," was the reply.

The boatswain's mate and the rescued man looked as if they did not quite understand. "You must know, sir," said the latter, doubtfully, "that all this beating and pounding was done on the high seas."

"Well, what of it? When one man, without any provocation, handles another as roughly as you have been handled, he is answerable to the law, no matter whether the offence was committed on the high seas or on the land."

"Come now, off you go, my man," said Uncle Dick. "The cutter is ready, and you've no time to lose. Yes, go with him and take charge of the boat, Lucas," he added, anticipating the request that the old boatswain's mate was about to make.

"And whatever you do, don't let those blubber-hunters catch you," said Eugene, in a low voice. He wanted to say it aloud, so that the cutter's crew could hear it; but knowing that Uncle Dick did not allow any interference with his men, he checked himself just in time.

The cutter's crew were all in their places, and there was a determined look on each man's face which said as plainly as words that the "blubber-hunters," even if they succeeded in overhauling them—which was not at all unlikely, seeing that the whale-boat was built for speed, and was pulled by a crew who were kept in excellent training by almost daily practice at the oars—the deserter should never be taken from them. Uncle Dick seemed to read the thoughts that were passing through their minds, and as he looked at the sturdy fellows, who had thrown off their caps and rolled up their sleeves in preparation for a long, hard pull, he remarked to Frank that he would not care to be in that whale-boat if she succeeded in coming up with the cutter.

CHAPTER III.

A SEA LAWYER.

THE cutter's bow swung away from the schooner
as soon as the boatswain's mate and the
rescued man were fairly seated, the oars dropped
into the water, and then began a race that promised
to be as exciting as even Eugene could have wished
it. The boys once more ran up the rigging, so that
they could watch both contestants. The whale-boat
certainly had the better crew, and, although she was
propelled by only five oars to the cutter's eight, she
seemed to move two feet to the other boat's one.
Especially was this the case when the man in gray,
who was standing in the stern-sheets holding the
steering-oar, became aware of what was going on.
As soon as he saw the cutter moving away from the
Stranger he comprehended the situation, and giving

utterance to some heavy adjectives, which by the time they came to the boys' ears sounded a good deal like oaths, ordered his crew to "Pick her up and run right along with her." They responded promptly, and sent their boat through the water at such a rate that Uncle Dick became uneasy at the prospect of a collision between her crew and the cutter's.

"I shouldn't think there would be any danger," said Frank. "There are eleven men in our boat, counting the deserter, and only six in his."

"But there is no officer in our boat," said Uncle Dick, "and this man being a captain, will expect our crew to obey his orders. I am really afraid he will be disappointed."

Frank, remembering the savage and determined expression he had seen on the face of every one of the cutter's crew, was quite sure he would be.

In a few minutes the whale-boat came close aboard the schooner, and dashed by under her bows. Her captain was furious, his face showed that. He ran his eye over the men on the

Stranger's deck, and picking out Uncle Dick at once as the commanding officer, said, as he nodded his head to him—

"Fine business you're in, sir! helping men to desert. If there is a law on shore I'll see you again, my good fellow!"

Uncle Dick simply smiled and touched his hat, and the whale-boat passed on. As she was going by, the sailors enacted a little pantomime of their own. They had clambered out on the bowsprit to see the race, and when the captain of the whaler was through threatening Uncle Dick, they glanced toward the quarter-deck, to make sure that none of their officers were observing them, and then leaned over and shook their fists at the angry man. One of them hugged his cap under his arm and beat it furiously with his clenched hand, nodding pleasantly to the captain the while, as if to indicate that it would have afforded him infinite satisfaction if the captain's head had been in the place of the cap. The boys, from their lofty perch in the main rigging, saw all that passed, and smiled at one another,

but said nothing; for they knew that if the performance came to the ears of Uncle Dick, who was a
very strict disciplinarian, every one of the sailors
who took part in it would be sent to the mast.*
Although he might laugh over it afterward in the
privacy of his cabin, he was not the one to pass
lightly over an insult to a shipmaster when in performance of his duty, no matter how great the
provocation.

All this while the cutter's crew had been exceedingly busy, and now loud calls were heard from the
boys on the cross-trees for their field-glasses. They
did not want to miss a single incident of the race.
Frank, who up to this time had remained below with
Uncle Dick, went into the cabin after the glasses,
and mounting the rigging, joined the group on the
cross-trees. "Who's ahead?" he asked.

---

* The "mast" is to a sailor on board ship, what the
"library" is to a refractory boy on shore. It is there that
culprits are sent to be reprimanded, if their offence be a
slight one, or sentenced if they have done something de-
serving of punishment.

" O, the cutter," replied George Le Dell. " There is more in that crew than I thought. They'll land their man safe enough."

And George was right. The cutter reached the wharf while the whale-boat was yet twenty yards away, and no sooner did she swing broadside to it than the deserter was lifted in the strong arms of the coxswain and boatswain's mate and fairly thrown ashore. He jumped to his feet and disappeared in less time than it takes to tell it. A few seconds later the whale-boat landed and the captain sprang out and started in pursuit, not, however, without saying a few words to the cutter's crew, which he emphasized by shaking his fist at them. If any of the men replied, our young friends at the cross-trees saw nothing to indicate it.

The sailors pulled back slowly, for their long, hard pull had wearied them, and when they reached the schooner and clambered over the side, the boys saw that their faces were flushed, and that some portions of their clothes looked as though they had been dipped in the bay. The boatswain's mate

went aft demurely enough to report the safe return
of the boat, but when he made his way forward
again, and glanced up at the boys, with whom he
was an especial favorite, they saw that his jolly
countenance was wreathed with smiles, and that his
broad shoulders were shaking with suppressed mirth.
He and the cutter's crew were proud of the exploit
they had performed. The fun and excitement
being all over now, the boys seated themselves in a
circle on the cross-trees to discuss the incidents
that had just transpired.

"Now just listen to me a moment, Frank, and
I'll ask you a question," said Perk. "Can that
brutal fellow do anything to Uncle Dick for assisting his man to escape?"

"If you should see me assaulted by ruffians who
were getting the better of me, and should rescue me
from their clutches, could they do anything to you
in law?" asked Frank, in reply.

"Certainly not."

"The same law holds good on the sea. Some
people have a very mistaken idea of things. They

insist on a landsman's right of self-defence, but deny the same to a sailor. Even sailors themselves think that because they follow the sea for a livelihood, they are debarred from exercising the very first law of our nature."

"Hear! hear!" cried Archie.

"Silence in the court-room!" exclaimed Featherweight, assuming a fierce frown. "Hurrah for free trade and sailors' rights, the motto on—on—somebody's flag! Proceed, brother Nelson. State the case to the jury."

Frank laughed as heartily as the rest for a few minutes, and continued:

"Sailors know that resistance to an officer, or even an attempt to spread dissatisfaction among the crew of a vessel, is called mutiny; and they know, too, that men have been hanged in the American navy for that very offence."

"See Cooper's Naval History for an account of the mutiny on board the United States brig-of-war Somers, in 1842," said Bab.

"That was the very circumstance I had in my

mind," returned Frank. "Sailors know all this, as I was saying, and consequently they are afraid to call their souls their own. They suffer in silence, unless they are driven to commit suicide during the voyage, and when they get ashore forget it all, or make a feeble attempt to punish their tyrants by process of law, but they soon give it up, for at the very outset they find an insurmountable obstacle in their way. Before they can convict they must prove three things—that the punishment they received was cruel and unusual; that it was inflicted without any just cause; and that the occasion of it was malice, hatred, or a desire for revenge on the part of the officer who punished them. Now, no living being can prove this last accusation against another, for in order to do it he must be able to read his fellow-men as he would an open book, and see what is passing in their minds; and even that would do him no good unless he possessed the power to make the judge and jury who try the case see the matter just as he does."

"Suppose this deserter could prove his complaints

against the master of that whaler," said Walter;
" what would be the penalty ?"

" One thousand dollars fine and five years in the
state prison."

" And I hope he will get it all," said Eugene.

" Well, if it is so hard for a seaman to obtain
satisfaction at law, what ought he to do when he is
abused at sea ?" asked Bab. " I understood you to
say he had two remedies, and you have given only
one."

" Well, there is another," said Frank. " He and
his companions ought to club together, take the ship
out of the hands of her officers, confine them in the
cabin, and make for the nearest port, if they are
navigators enough to find their way there."

" Yes," exclaimed Archie, " and swing for it the
moment they reach the shore."

" No, sir. The case has been tried in the courts
more than once, and would be tried oftener if sailors
only knew their rights. As far as any risk I might
run is concerned, I would not be afraid to belong to
such a crew and take part in just such a proceeding."

4

"Well, I don't want you to get into any such scrape," said Archie; "I should never expect to see you again."

"I have no desire to win notoriety as a mutineer, I assure you," replied Frank, with a laugh. "As his Honor remarked"—here he waved his hand towards Featherweight, who bowed gravely—"I was only discoursing on sailors' rights."

"There," said George, as the boatswain's whistle rang through the schooner, followed by the order, given in a very hoarse voice, "Away, you gigs, away!"—"the captain is going ashore. Hadn't we better go down and keep Dick Lewis and Bob company? The old fellows will be lonely."

"That means business," said Eugene. "Uncle Dick is going ashore to see about the stores. It will not be long now before we take leave of Fr'isco."

"And what will be our next port?" asked George.

This was something that had not yet been decided, and if one might judge by what the boys said while they were descending to the deck, there was a prospect of a lively debate if the matter were left to them. Eugene wanted to go straight to Alaska. Bab, who had lately been reading "Reindeer, Dogs and Snow-shoes," was in favor of that, provided they could afterward go across to some port in Siberia and stay there long enough to see a little of the wild life in which he had been so much interested. Perk would agree to all that, in case they could stop on the way and give him a chance to try his hand at salmon-fishing in the tributaries of the Columbia river. Fred had seen quite enough of snow and ice, and thought he could have more sport in a warm country. He wanted to go to Japan. Walter said he was strongly in favor of that, for after they had seen all the sights in that country they would probably go to India, and that was what he wanted. He was impatient to ride on an elephant and see the famous Indian jugglers and serpent-charmers. Every boy wanted to go somewhere, but the trouble was that no two of them wanted to go to the same place; and Frank wondered how the matter would be decided. How astonished he would have been to know that the man in gray, who had just gone by in the whale-boat, was destined to decide it for them!

The boys spent the rest of the day in company with the trappers. Nothing more was said on the subject which had for a long time been uppermost in their minds, for the tone in which Dick's answer had been given satisfied them that it was final. The boys were all sorry, for they had become greatly attached to these two good-natured, ignorant fellows. They had been of great service to them— beyond a doubt they had saved Walter's life—and they could not but miss them when they were gone. The cousins especially would have been glad to postpone the parting moment had they possessed the power. It was not at all likely that they would ever see the mountains or the prairie again, and even if they did, the chances that they would find their old friends, the trappers, were not one in a thousand. Their meeting with them had been purely accidental this time, and it was not probable that such a combination of circumstances would ever occur again.

About supper-time Uncle Dick returned and reported that all arrangements had been made. The schooner was to be hauled alongside the dock in the morning, and they would go out with the turn of the tide. Where were they going? He didn't care. The world was before them, and when the boys had made up their minds what portion of it they wanted to see first, they could come to him with their decision. He wasn't going to bother his head about it, for he had other matters to think of. Eight o'clock the next evening would see the Stranger under way, and if the boys had any business ashore they had better attend to it the first thing in the morning.

Uncle Dick retired at an early hour, as he always did, and the boys had the quarter-deck all to themselves until eleven o'clock—or rather they had it in company with the second mate and the quartermaster on watch. A few " primary meetings" had been held immediately after supper, but they amounted to nothing. Each boy knew upon whom he could rely to second any motion he might make, but he was not so certain of the number of votes he could raise in support of it. During the two hours' conversation that took place after Uncle Dick went to bed, Fred Craven arose six times— that is, once every twenty minutes—and said gravely,

"I move you, Mr. President, that the captain of this schooner be requested to take her directly to some port in Japan."

"I second the motion," said Frank, who was speaking for Walter.

"Gentlemen, you have heard the motion," said Walter. "Are you ready for the question?"

"Mr. President," said Eugene, "I move to amend by striking out Japan and substituting Alaska."

"Second the motion," said Bab.

"You have heard the amendment. Are you ready to take action upon it?"

"Now just listen to me a minute, Mr. President, and I'll tell you what's a fact," said Perk. "I move to amend by striking out Alaska and substituting Astoria in Oregon."

"I second the motion," said George, who, being a devoted disciple of old Izaac Walton, was as fond of fishing as he was of sailing.

"Mr. President," said Archie, "I move to amend——"

"The gentleman is out of order. An amendment to an amendment is proper, but not an amendment of an amendment to an amendment."

When affairs reached this pass a hearty roar of laughter would come up through the open cabin windows, showing that there was an interested and amused listener in the person of Uncle Dick, who having gone to bed, leaving his state-room door ajar, could hear all that was said. Then speeches were made, some long and others witty, and all showing the training the boys had received in their debating societies. Eugene was particularly long-winded. According to Featherweight "he talked all manner of what," and spouted away on subjects that had not the slightest connection with the question under discussion. He talked eloquently about the American eagle, the war of 1812, and the stars and stripes, and dwelt long on the rights of sailors and other free-born citizens. He said afterward that if he couldn't gain his point any other way, he would tire his audience out, and compel them to vote for his amendment just to get rid of him. But the boys listened patiently and without once interrupting him, except by applause when he grew particularly eloquent, and the young orator finally tired himself out and took his seat in disgust. Everything was voted down; so they were no nearer a decision than they were before. There was one point, however, on which they were all agreed when the meeting broke up at eleven o'clock, and that was, that they had enjoyed themselves, and that their jaws and sides would be sure to ache for a week to come.

During the afternoon the boys had held a consultation with the boatswain's mate, who had promised to take the trappers under his especial charge during the night, and to report the first man who attempted to play any tricks upon them. After the meeting broke up the boys went forward with their friends to see them safely stowed away in the forecastle. The sailors were all up and waiting for them—not a man had yet turned in. The best bunks in the forecastle had been given up for their use, and the beds that were made up in them would have looked very inviting to almost anybody except our two back-woodsmen. Having been all their lives accustomed to sleeping on the hard ground, with nothing but a blanket or the spreading branches of some friendly tree for protection, they wanted plenty of air and elbow-room. They hesitated when they looked into the little forecastle, and drew back and shook their heads when invited to enter. Archie finally effected a compromise by bringing up a couple of blankets and spreading them on the deck near the windlass. This being perfectly satisfactory, the boys bade the trappers good-night, and went away, leaving them to the tender mercies of the sailors.

There was not much sleeping done among those foremast hands that night. They did not play any tricks upon their guests—indeed there were not many among them who would have had the hardihood to attempt it, after taking a good look at the stalwart fellows—but they crammed them "chock-a-block" with such wild stories of the sea that the trappers grew more alarmed than ever, and wondered greatly at the recklessness of the men who would willingly encounter such dangers. They told about mermaids, sea-dragons and serpents; of Vanderdecker's ghostly ship, the Flying Dutchman, which was rushing about the ocean with the speed of a railroad train, running down and sinking every craft that came in her way; of monstrous cuttle-fish which would sometimes arise suddenly out of the depths, and twining their long arms about a ship, sink with it and all the crew to the bottom; and one of the men declared that he had actually met and been swallowed by the same whale that took Jonah in out of the wet, hundreds and thousands of years before, and to prove it, exhibited the tobacco-box which had dropped out of Jonah's pocket when the whale threw him ashore. This is a staple forecastle yarn, and every one who has had an hour's conversation with a sailor, has probably heard it; but it was new to the trappers, who listened with all their ears and with unmistakable signs of terror on their faces. The simple-hearted fellows believed every word, and when the conversation lagged for a moment, spoke of the magnet Eugene had shown them, and the use for which they supposed it was intended.

This started the sailors on a new tack, and the stories that followed were more wonderful than those which had just been told. There was not a sailor on board the Stranger who had not seen some unlucky vessel tumble off the under side of the earth, her magnet proving too weak to sustain her weight; and there were two or three who had belonged to the crews of those very vessels, and who had been saved by a miracle.

The night was passed in this way, and it was daylight before the trappers lay down on their blankets to rest, but not to sleep. They could not sleep after hearing of such wonderful adventures and talking face to face with the men who had taken part in them. If they had not already made up their minds to lose no time in seeking safety among their native mountains, they would have done so now.

CHAPTER IV.

"SHANGHAIED."

THE morning broke-bright and clear, and all hands were astir at an early hour. The first thing was to hoist the anchor and haul the schooner alongside the dock. This being done, breakfast was served, and the boys having put on their shore-clothes, started out to take a good look at the city which they might never see again, and to make purchases of various articles they needed. Fred and Eugene each wanted a rifle and a brace of revolvers, their own weapons having been stolen from them by the hunters who robbed the Pike. Some of the others needed a few articles of clothing, and Frank's Maynard required some repairs. They set out together, but before an hour had passed, were scattered all over the city. Fred, Archie and Eugene hired a carriage and went for a ride, taking old Bob with them, while Dick Lewis stuck close to Frank and Walter. Knowing that the time for parting was not far distant, he did not seem willing to allow them out of his sight.

A few years before men like Dick were often met with in the streets of the city; but now a genuine trapper was not seen every day, and he created something of a sensation wherever he went. Almost every one he met stared at him and turned to look at him after he had passed; and Dick, finally becoming nettled by the interest and curiosity his appearance excited, begged the boys to take him back to the schooner and leave him there. He would stay on board until she was ready to sail, he said, and then he and Bob would bid a long farewell to civilization, and make the best of their way back to Fort Bolton. He hoped that neither of them would ever see a paved street or a brick house again.

At six o'clock in the evening the boys, and the few sailors who had been allowed shore liberty, began to retrace their steps toward the dock where the Stranger was lying. At seven they were all on board except two—Lucas, the boatswain's mate, and Barton, the coxswain of the cutter. These men had not been seen since noon, and they were to have been back at three o'clock. Preparations were already being made for getting under way, and Uncle Dick began to grow impatient. "I don't see what keeps those fellows," said he to Frank. "I have always found them trustworthy, and I hope they will not fail me now."

"I must go ashore again after my rifle, you know," replied Frank—"it was to be done at half-past seven—and I'll go along the dock and keep an eye out for them."

"All right. Hurry them up, if you see them, and be sure that you are in time yourself."

Frank went ashore accompanied by the trapper—Dick was not afraid of attracting so much attention now that it was growing dark—and hurried away toward the gunsmith's. He followed the wharves as long as they led him in the direction he wanted to go, looking everywhere for the missing sailors, but without finding them. The actions of himself and his companion attracted the attention of two men, who were walking along the dock behind them. They watched them for some time, and then, after whispering together a few minutes, one of them came up and tapped Frank on the shoulder. "Who are you looking for?" said he.

Frank turned and fastening his eyes on the man took a good survey of him before he answered. He was a flashily-dressed person, with a sneaking, hang-dog cast of countenance, and the grimy hand he placed upon Frank's shoulder, and which the latter promptly shook off, was heavily loaded with bogus jewelry.

"Don't be quite so familiar, if you please!" said Frank.

"Beg pardon," said the man, stepping back and straightening up his battered plug hat which he had thus far worn cocked over his left ear. "I thought you belonged to the Stranger."

"And what if I do?" asked Frank.

" I thought maybe you were looking for them two
men."

" What two men ?"

" Why, one of 'em is a short, thick-set fellow, and
carries a silver whistle in the breast pocket of his
shirt. The other is tall and slender, wears some
kind of a badge on his arm—a petty officer's badge
I took it to be—and has light hair and whiskers."

The man gave an accurate description of the
missing sailors of whom Frank was in search. No
doubt they had got into trouble and found their way
into some station-house ; and this fellow was some
little pettifogger, who hoped to make a few dollars
by helping them out.

" I thought maybe you were looking for 'em,"
continued the man, as he turned to go away ;
" but seeing you ain't, I am sorry I pestered you."

" One moment, please," said Frank. " Where
are these men now ?"

" They're aboard my ship."

" O, you're a sailor, are you ?" exclaimed Frank,
again running his eye over the man, who looked

5

about as much like a sailor as Dick Lewis did. "What is the name of your ship, and where is she?"

"She's the Sunrise, and she is at anchor out here in the bay."

"How came our men aboard of her?"

"Well, you see, they've got some friends and acquaintances among my crew, and when we were lying alongside the dock they came aboard to see them.. While they were skylarking about, one of them, the boatswain, fell into the hold and broke his leg. We hauled out into the bay just after that, and did it in such a hurry—you see there was another ship waiting to take our berth at the dock as soon as we were out of it—that we didn't have time to put him ashore. We've had a doctor to see him, and maybe it would be a good plan to get an ambulance and take him back where he belongs."

"I think so too," said Frank, who became interested at once; "that is, if he can bear removal. But whatever we do, must be done at once. Our vessel is all ready to sail."

"I guess he can stand it to be moved. You

might come aboard and see—you and your pardner here. I've got a boat close by."

Frank assenting to this proposition, he and Dick Lewis followed the man, who led the way along the wharf, and finally showed them a yawl manned by two oarsmen. They climbed down into it, their companion took his seat at the helm, and the boat was pushed off into the darkness. The man talked incessantly, answering all Frank's questions, and going so fully into the particulars of the accident that had befallen the boatswain's mate, and telling so straight and reasonable a story, that not a shadow of a doubt entered Frank's mind. He remarked that the ship was a long way from the wharf, and that the two men who were pulling the oars looked more like "dock rats" than sailors; but still he scarcely bestowed a second thought upon these matters, for his mind was fully occupied with the injured man to whose relief he was hastening. At last the hull and rigging of a ship loomed up through the darkness, and a hoarse voice hailed the yawl.

" Sunrise !" replied the man at the helm.

The answer was perfectly right and proper. It conveyed to them on board the ship the information that their captain was in the approaching boat; but it seemed to Frank that his presence brought very little show of respect from the officer in charge of the deck, for he ordered no lanterns to light him aboard. Indeed there were no lights to be seen on the deck, as Frank found when he clambered over the side, the only ones visible being those in the rigging, which were placed there to point out the position of the ship, so that passing vessels might not run into her.

The captain, who was the first to board the ship, talked rapidly in a low tone to some one who hurried aft to meet him, and when Frank came up, he said aloud :—

"Take this gentleman into the forecastle and give him all the help he needs to remove that man. This one," he added, pointing to Dick, "can go with a couple of you to get a stretcher."

"Ay! ay! sir," replied a voice. "Step right this way, sir."

Frank followed the speaker toward the forecastle, and when he came within sight of the ladder that led into it, was surprised to see that it was as dark as a dungeon below. Then for the first time the thought that things did not look just right began to creep through his mind. His companion descended the ladder, but Frank halted at the top. "Look here, my friend," said he; "if you want to get me below there you had better light up first."

"Come on," said the man, in a tone of command.

"Where's that sailor with the broken leg?" demanded Frank.

"Are you going to come on?" asked the man.

"Well, that depends——I want to hear from that man of ours first. If you are down there, Lucas, sing out!"

There was no response. In an instant it flashed upon Frank that he and Dick had been led into a trap. The man in the battered plug hat was no captain at all. Probably he was a shipping-agent. Having persuaded Frank and the trapper to accompany him on board the ship, he made a very plausible excuse for separating them for a moment, so that they could not assist each other, and now they were to be overpowered and confined until the vessel was well out to sea, when they would be brought out and compelled to act with the crew. While Frank was thinking about it, his conductor, who had gone half way down the ladder, turned around and started to come back. Frank's ears told him this and not his eyes, for they were of no use to him in that intense darkness. "Avast, there!" he cried, with emphasis. "If you come a step nearer to me I'll send you down that ladder quicker than you ever went down before. You have picked up the wrong men this time. Where is that scoundrel who called himself the master of this ship?"

"Here I am," replied that worthy, in tones very different from those he had thus far used in addressing Frank.

"Well, if you are wise, you will undo this half-hour's work with the least possible delay. Call away that boat and leave us a clear road to get to it, or——"

Frank was interrupted by the sounds of a fierce struggle which just then arose from the quarter-deck. He heard the sound of stamping and scraping feet, muttered oaths and blows, and then Dick's voice rang out clear above the tumult. "Keep off, the hul on you," said he, "fur I'm a leetle wusser nor a hul parsel of wild-cats!" And then followed a sound such as might be made by somebody's head coming in violent contact with the deck.

"Stand your ground, Dick!" shouted Frank. "I'll be there in a minute!"

With these words he sprang forward, intending to run to his friend's assistance; but before he had made half a dozen steps his heels flew up and he was sent at full length on the deck, which he no sooner touched than two men, whom he had not yet seen, sprang up from behind the windlass and threw themselves across his shoulders. He had been entirely deceived as to the number of enemies with whom he had to deal. He had seen but four men on deck and there proved to be a dozen of them —more than enough to render resistance useless.

Almost before he realized the fact he was powerless, a pair of irons being slipped over his wrists and another about his ankles. When he was helped to his feet, he found that the struggle on the quarter-deck had ended in the same way. Dick Lewis was led up, and by the light of a lantern which one of the crew drew from under a tarpaulin, Frank saw that he was ironed like himself.

The man who carried the lantern held it up so that its rays fell full on the prisoners, and gave them a good looking over, bestowing his attentions principally upon their arms and shoulders, as if trying to judge of the amount of muscle they might contain. "They'll do," said he, at last, "and now we're all ready to be off. Can you pull an oar?" he added, flashing his lantern in Frank's face.

"I can," was the reply.

"I can! Is that the way you talk to me? I am mate of this vessel and there's a handle to my name."

"I did not know that you were an officer," replied

Frank, "ånd neither am I aware that I am under any obligations to put a handle to your name."

"Well, you'll find it out pretty sudden. It shall be my first hard work to teach you manners, my fine gentleman. Take 'em below."

The mate handed the lantern to one of the crew, who moved toward the forecastle, followed by the prisoners, who never uttered a word of complaint or remonstrance. Frank knew it would do no good, and Dick was so bewildered that he could not have spoken if he had tried. He kept as close to his young companion as he could. He seemed to think that Frank, powerless as he was, could in some way protect him. They followed their conductor into the forecastle, and the latter, after hanging the lantern to one of the carlens, went on deck again, closing the hatch after him.

Frank and the trapper looked about them before they spoke. The very first objects their eyes rested on were the two missing seamen, the coxswain and the boatswain's mate, who lay side by side in one of the bunks, snoring at the rate of ten knots an hour. They were there, sure enough—the bogus captain told the truth on that point—and Frank was glad to see that they were all right, or would be as soon as the effects of the drug they had swallowed had been slept off. There were three other men in the forecastle, and they were in irons like themselves. They lay in their bunks and looked sullenly at the new-comers. "What's the matter with you?" asked Frank. "What have you been doing to get yourselves in this fix?"

"Trying to desert," growled one of the sailors, in reply. "What's the matter with *you?*"

"Shanghaied," answered Frank. "What ship is this, and where is she bound?"

"She's the Tycoon, and I expect she's off for the Japan station."

Frank's heart seemed to stop beating. His situation was even worse than he had supposed. He recalled the story of the man he had seen desert that same ship on that very day, and shuddered when he thought of what might be in store for him.

"What did you say was the matter with us, Master

Frank?" asked the trapper, leaning against a bunk by his friend's side and speaking in a low voice.

"I say we have been shanghaied—that is, kidnapped," replied Frank.

"But what fur?" said Dick, who did not understand the matter at all. "We hain't been a doin' of nothing."

"I know that; but you see—in the first place, Dick, there's no use in denying that we are in serious trouble. You might as well know it first as last and make up your mind to stand it, for there is no way of escape. This is the same ship that that man we picked up to-day deserted from, and that red-faced man in gray whom we saw in the whale-boat is the captain of her. He and his officers treat their men so harshly that they run away every chance they get. The captain must have men to handle his vessel, and as he can't get them in the regular way, he kidnaps them."

"But what do I know 'bout a ship?" exclaimed Dick.

"Nothing whatever; but that is no matter. You

have good strong arms, and it will not take long to break you in."

"Whar—whar——"

The trapper could not ask the question he was most anxious to have answered. It seemed to stick in his throat.

"I know what you mean," said Frank. "This man says we are bound for Japan, and that is nearly three thousand miles from here."

Dick was frightened almost out of his senses. His face grew as pale as death, great drops of perspiration stood on his forehead, and he tugged and pulled at his irons with the strength of desperation. But they had been put on him to stay, and all his efforts to free himself were unavailing. Frank knew what he stood in fear of, and he knew, too, that anything he could say would not set the poor fellow's mind at rest. The wrong ideas he had formed of things and the ridiculous stories he had heard in the forecastle of the Stranger, had made an impression on him so deep and lasting that even Frank, in whom the trapper had every confidence, could not remove it. The real dangers he was likely to encounter would be but small things comparatively ; but the imaginary evils which he would look for every day, would cause him much suffering. Frank thought more of his friend than he did of himself. How would Dick behave when he found himself dancing over the waves of the Pacific in a small boat in pur-- suit of a whale ? What would he think if he saw one of those monsters of the deep—as Lucas, the boat-swain's mate, said he had often seen them—come up on a breach, shoot up forty or fifty feet into the air, and then fall down into the water with a noise like the roar of Niagara ? No doubt he would refuse duty. No doubt, too, when the captain or his officers attempted to punish him for disobedience there would be a desperate fight —for Dick stood not in fear of anything that walked on two feet—which would not end until the trapper had been severely injured and perhaps permanently disabled.

"Human natur'! What'll I do?" cried Dick, after he had exhausted himself in his efforts to pull off his irons.

"Watch me and do as I do, as nearly as you can," replied Frank. "We are completely in the power of these men, and there is no way to get out of it. While on our voyage from Bellville, I took particular pains to learn all I could of a seaman's duties, and perhaps I shall be able to be of some assistance to you. What we don't know Lucas and Barton will teach us. But, whatever you do, don't refuse duty or talk back, no matter what is said or done to you. It will only be worse for you if you do."

"And bear another thing in mind," said one of the sailors, who had been listening to this conversation, "and that is, you take rank next below the cap'n's dog, and hain't got no rights of your own!"

The trapper looked toward Frank, and while the latter was explaining that, according to a sailor's creed, those who follow the sea take rank in this way: first the captain, then the mates, then the captain's dog, and lowest of all, the foremast hands—while Frank was explaining this, there was the sound of a commotion on the deck over their heads, and after listening a moment the sailors declared that the vessel was about to be taken to sea. And so it proved. The anchor was hove up, the sails spread one after the other, and finally the prisoners below began to feel the increasing motion of the ship. Just then the hatch was thrown open and the first mate came down the ladder. He walked straight up to Dick, unlocked his irons and slapping him on the back ordered him to go on deck and lend a hand. Even this simple order was Greek to the honest trapper; but he understood the word "go," and he went, delighted to find himself in possession of his liberty once more. Frank would have been glad to go with him, for it was anything but agreeable to his feelings to be confined below like a felon; but the officers wanted to get a little farther away from shore before they allowed too many of their unwilling crew the free use of their hands and feet.

The first order Dick heard when he reached the deck was : "Let fall and sheet home;" and the mate giving him a push by the shoulder and a kick at the same time, commanded him to "Grab hold of that rope and pull as if the sweetheart he left in the backwoods was at the other end of it." Or, we ought rather say that that was the order the mate intended to give, but he never finished it, for he was knocked down so promptly that it seemed as if his foot and the trapper's right arm were both put in motion at the same instant. Dick's hot blood, which was already at fever heat, boiled over completely when he felt the weight of the mate's boot, and he wiped out the insult as soon as it was given.

Of course there was a tumult at once. The second mate caught up a handspike and the captain descended from his quarter-deck, flourishing a rope's end as he came. They advanced upon the trapper from opposite sides, but he was ready and waiting, and they must have been astonished at the rough reception they met at his hands. With one single twist, which was so sudden and powerful that it almost dislocated the second mate's shoulder, Dick wrenched the handspike out of his grasp and threw it to the deck. Then his long arms swung in the air like the shafts of a windmill, one huge clenched hand, as heavy as a sledgehammer, fell full in the captain's face, the other alighted on the top of the mate's head, and both these worthies sank to the deck on the instant.

The first mate by this time recovered his feet, and picking up a handspike looked all around for the trapper ; but he was not to be seen anywhere on deck. Nor indeed was he to be found about the ship. He was gone.

6

CHAPTER V.

THE TRAPPER'S ADVENTURE.

WHAT time is it now, Eugene?"

"Just nine o'clock. What do you suppose is the matter, Uncle?"

"I wish I knew. They are all of them old enough and large enough to take care of themselves, but I can't help thinking that there's something wrong."

"I have half a mind to go ashore and look for them."

"I don't know what good that would do. You don't know where to look, and if they should happen to come aboard while you were gone, we should have to send some one in search of you, and that would cause another delay."

The stores were all aboard, the Stranger was ready to sail, and had been for more than an hour, but three of her company were missing, and so was the trapper. Uncle Dick and the boys had been impatient at first, but this gradually gave way to a feeling of uneasiness and anxiety. Everybody had some explanation to offer for Frank's absence, and the prevailing opinion seemed to be that the sailors, having got themselves into trouble during the day, had been arrested, and that Frank was trying to effect their release. Old Bob was more uneasy than the rest, and couldn't make up his mind what to think about it, not knowing the dangers which one might encounter while roaming about the city after dark. His kit and Dick's were packed and lying at the head of the companion-way, and the old fellow was in a hurry to be off. Had they been in the mountains the trapper's absence would have caused him no anxiety. There Dick knew all about things, and was abundantly able to take care of number one; but in the settlements he was like a child, and almost as incapable of looking out for himself. Old Bob was afraid something had happened to him or Frank, and the others began to think so too as the hours

wore away and their missing friends did not appear.
Uncle Dick finally gave up all hopes of seeing them
that night, and ordering one watch below, went to
bed himself, leaving instructions with the officer of
the deck to call him the moment Frank arrived.
The impatient boys remained on deck an hour or
two longer; but at last they also grew weary and
turned in and went to sleep.

Just at daylight they were awakened by hasty
steps on the companion-ladder, and the officer of the
watch hurried into the cabin and pounded loudly on
the captain's door. "Ay! ay!" replied Uncle Dick.

"That trapper is coming back, sir," said the
officer, "and he's having a fuss out there on the dock."

"He is having what?" asked Uncle Dick.

"He's in a rumpus of some kind, sir. He's got
somebody on his back and is lugging him along as
if he were a bag of potatoes."

"It isn't Captain Nelson or one of the men, is it?"
asked Uncle Dick, anxiously.

"O no, sir. It is a landsman and a stranger."

This conversation was carried on in a tone of

voice loud enough to be heard by all the boys, who were out on the floor in an instant. It was but a few seconds' work to jump into their trowsers and boots, and catch up their coats and hats, and they were on deck almost as soon as the officer himself. A strange sight met their eyes. A short distance up the dock was Dick Lewis, running at the top of his speed, and carrying on his shoulder a man almost as large as himself, who kicked and struggled in vain to escape from the strong grasp that held him. The load was undoubtedly a heavy one, but the trapper moved with it plenty fast enough to leave behind two ill-looking fellows, who carried bludgeons in their hands, and who were trying to overtake him. About two hundred yards farther up the dock were two more men, one supporting the other, who was limping along half doubled up as if in great pain.

The boys, wondering greatly, sprang ashore and ran up the wharf to meet Dick. The latter, to quote from Featherweight, looked as though he had been somewhere. His buckskin suit, soaked with water, clung close to his person ; his hat was gone, and his face wore an expression that the old members of the club had never seen there before. Archie had seen it, however, and that was on the day when, seated at the camp-fire near the Old Bear's Hole, years before, Frank related to himself and Uncle James the particulars of his meeting with Black Bill and his party, and the manner in which he had been treated by them.

Dick grinned the delight he felt at meeting the boys once more, but did not stop to speak to them. He went straight on board the schooner and threw off his burden, at the same time seizing his man by the collar and jerking him upon his feet in front of Uncle Dick Gaylord, who looked at him in amazement.

"Here's the mean chap that done it all," said the trapper, throwing his full strength into his arm and giving the bogus captain—for it was he—such a shaking that his teeth fairly rattled. "Now if thar's any law in the settlements set it a-going."

"What did he do?" demanded the boys, who had followed close at his heels. "Where's Frank?"

"He's round on the other side of the 'arth by this time, I reckon," replied Dick, drawing his hand across his forehead and looking about as if he were overjoyed to find himself among friends once more.

"I hope they've got a horse-shoe big enough to hold 'em on, but I'm 'most afeard, 'cause she's a heap bigger nor this little boat o' your'n."

"What is?" asked the captain, and the boys grew anxious when they saw the expression that settled on his face. "Begin at the beginning and tell us all about it."

Thus adjured, the trapper launched at once into his story, without wasting any time in explanatory remarks, and for ten minutes held his auditors spellbound. He told how he and Frank had been enticed on board the Tycoon, described the manner in which they had been overpowered and confined, repeated the conversation that took place between Frank and himself in the forecastle, and ended by relating the particulars of his "scrimmage" with the officers of the ship, with all of which the reader is already acquainted; but he does not know what happened afterward, so from this point we will tell the story in our own words.

The reason Dick could not be found on board the ship after his fight with the officers was ended, was because he was not there—he had jumped overboard; and what was rather singular, none of the crew on deck had seen him when he did it. The last time they saw him he was clambering into one of the bow-boats, and that was the first place they looked for him, his concealment being pointed out to the officers by a man who was looked upon as the "black sheep" of the crew, and of whom we shall probably hear more as our story progresses. But when the officers came to search the boat, Dick was not there; he had dropped unseen into the water.

The trapper was a famous swimmer, and entertained no doubt of his ability to reach the shore; but even had the vessel been twenty miles at sea, he would have trusted himself to the waves rather than run the risk of encountering the terrible dangers that awaited the ship and her crew on the "under side of the earth." The worst thing he would have to contend with in case he were recaptured, would be the tyranny of the captain and his brutal officers; but the sturdy trapper gave not one thought to that, for during a life of excitement and adventure he had more than once demonstrated his ability to protect himself; but he *did* think of that ghostly ship, the Flying Dutchman, the big cuttle-fish, the mermaids and sea-dragons, the whale that swallowed Jonah, and which was still roaming about seeking whom he might devour, and, worse than all, the awful danger of the ship falling off when she came to the under side of the earth and was sailing along with her masts pointing downward and the crew walking with their feet upward. Dick thought of all these dangers and swam as if he saw them looming up close behind him; but with all his exertions he could not make headway fast enough to suit him. His wet clothing hung upon him like lead and deadened his progress through the water; so the first thing he did when the ship was out of sight, was to stop and relieve himself of this encumbrance. He took off moccasins and all, and wrapping them up in his hunting-shirt put the bundle on his back and tied it around his neck with the sleeves of the shirt. After that he made better headway.

It is hard to tell what would have been the result of the trapper's adventure, had it not been for some assistance which fortunately came in his way. Had there been light enough so that he could see to direct his course, the swim would have been nothing; but there was danger of moving in a circle in the darkness, and so tiring himself out without making any headway at all. There were no lights in front to guide him, but there were some behind, and after looking at them two or three times the swimmer became convinced that they were coming toward him. There was a vessel of some kind approaching, and Dick, changing his course a little to intercept her, had the satisfaction of hearing his hail answered, and of seeing the little fishing-smack which carried the lights thrown up into the wind within a few yards of him.

"Hello, there!" cried a gruff voice.

"Hello, you!" shouted Dick. "Here I am."

"Well, what do you want?" asked the captain of the fishing boat, peering out into the darkness and trying to discover whence the hail came.

"Is civilized folks human enough to lend a sufferin' feller-man a helpin' hand?" asked Dick, who after his recent experience had some serious doubts on this point.

This question was not immediately answered, for the skipper did not quite understand it. He held a consultation with one of his men and then called out—

"If you want help, pull this way. I've got no boat to send out after you!"

Dick was pulling that way with all his might, and guided by the lanterns that were held over the side, at last reached the boat, which sat so low in the water that he could lay hold of her rail. The astonishment of her crew as they hauled aboard a man who carried all his wearing apparel around his neck, was unbounded. They gave him time to put on his clothes and then directed him to the captain who was waiting to see him.

The very first question that gentleman propound-
ed to him aroused a thousand fears in Dick's mind.
The skipper wanted to know where he came from,
and how he happened to be out there in the water,
five miles from land; and the trapper, fearful that if
he told the truth and acknowledged himself to be a
deserter, the captain might follow the Tycoon and
compel him to go aboard of her again, whether he
wanted to or not, did something he had never done
before—he made up a story all out of his own head,
as he told Uncle Dick Gaylord, and queer work he
made of it. He entered into the particulars of a
fearful shipwreck that had just occurred. The waves
were as high as the Rocky Mountains, he said, the
wind blew so hard that the sailors had to stop all
work and hold their hair on (this was a quotation
from one of the stories the trapper had heard in
the forecastle of the Stranger); his ship was cap-
sized no less than three times, always coming right
side up again, and doing it so quickly that she did
not even wet her sails or her deck, and none of the
crew had a chance to drop off into the water (another

quotation); but finally the wind came in such furious
gusts that it took the masts right out by the roots
(still another quotation), and the ship filled and went
down like lead. The trapper said that all this happened not five minutes before, and that set the crew
of the fishing-boat into a roar of laughter, for they had
been out all day, and knew there had scarcely been
wind enough to raise any white caps. The captain
used some hard words, and called Dick anything
but a truthful man; but the latter affirmed so solemnly that it was all so, that the skipper thought
that perhaps something had happened after all, and
spent a long time in cruising about the place where
Dick had been picked up.

This delay added to the trapper's fears. What
if the Tycoon should come back in search of him?
Alarmed by the thought, he labored hard to convince
the captain that every soul on board the wrecked
ship, except himself, had gone down with her;
but finding that the skipper paid no attention to
him, he changed his story altogether, and declared
that he had jumped overboard on purpose, and that

he had done it because he had taken passage on the wrong vessel. He wanted to go to Sacramento, he said, but by mistake had boarded a craft bound for the "under side of the earth;" and as she would not turn back and put him ashore, he had no alternative but to take to the water and get back as best he could. Then the skipper was angry in earnest. Ordering Dick to get as far forward as the length of the little vessel would allow, and not to open his head again as long as he remained on board of her, he filled away for the city.

The trapper was very glad to be let off so easily. He had induced the captain to turn his vessel toward the shore, and that was all he cared for. He crouched down in the bow and meekly submitted to the jokes and tricks of the sailors, who never allowed him a moment's peace. He was too completely cowed to take offence at anything. He had seen enough of civilized life and people to take all the courage out of him.

The moment the fishing boat touched the dock he was out and ashore. Then he was himself again.

When he felt something solid under his feet his courage all returned, and he was in just the right mood to carry out the exploit he afterward performed. Almost the first man he saw on the dock was the bogus captain, who had enticed Frank and himself on board the Tycoon. Dick's blood began to boil as soon as his eyes rested on him. His first thought was to take summary vengeance on him, but he was checked in time by the reflection that he was not in the mountains now, and that there were laws in the settlements strong enough to punish evil-doers of every description. He did not know how to set the law in motion, but the captain of the Stranger did, and he would take the culprit before him at once.

The bogus captain, whose business was that of shipping-agent and boarding-house keeper, was standing in the midst of a group of friends, half a dozen of them perhaps, and all men like himself; but this did not deter the trapper, who strode up and confronted him. The talking and laughing were hushed at once, and all eyes were turned upon the new-comer, who stood before them with dripping garments, his tall figure drawn up to its full height, his eyes flashing and his bony fingers working nervously. He looked dangerous. The bogus captain stared at him a moment doubtfully and then a gleam of intelligence crossed his face and he tried to smile.

"Why, I thought I had seen you before," said he, thrusting out his hand. "Come in! come right into the house. Where you been?"

"Whar do you reckon you seed me last?" demanded Dick, holding his arms behind his back, for the man seemed determined to shake hands with him whether he wished it or not. "You can't shut up my eyes with none of your palaverin', now. Whar do you reckon you seed me last, I axes you?"

"Why, let me think a minute," said the man, pulling off his plug hat and digging his fingers into his head, at the same time backing away from the enraged giant. "I see so many of you fellows that I can't call you all by name the minute I meet you."

"My name's—my name's——" Dick stopped and looked all around, trying to think what he should call himself. He did not have a very extensive

circle of acquaintances, and he could't make up a
name "all out of his own head," as he made up the
story he told the captain of the fishing-smack. "My
name's Colonel Gaylord," said he, giving the first
one that came into his mind.

"Ah! yes; I know you now," said the bogus
captain, making another effort to take the trapper
by the hand. "You're the chap I found a good
berth for a few days ago, ain't you? Seems to me—
you know——"

"Yes," roared Dick, who could control himself
no longer, "I know, an' 'tain't likely I'll ever forget,
nuther. I'm the man you wanted to send round to
the other side of the 'arth, to be chawed up by whales
an' dropped off into the clouds, consarn you—that's
who *I* am, an' you'll remember me afore you see the
last of me, I tell you. Human natur'! I wish I
could tote you out to the mountains fur about ten
minutes. But I'll set the law a-goin' agin you afore
you see another day; that's what I'll do. Come
along here, you meanest man the 'arth ever saw,
not even exceptin' Black Bill—come along! Stand

7

out o' the way, the rest on you, or I'll claw you all up like a painter!"

With these words the trapper seized the bogus captain by the collar and began pushing him toward the Stranger, which he could see still lying in her berth where he had left her. The man remonstrated and threatened, but all to no purpose. Then he resisted and called upon his companions for help. One of them responded, but was disposed of so quickly and effectually that the others thought it best to keep at a safe distance.

Finding that his man was possessed of more strength, activity and determination than he had calculated on, the trapper seized him with both hands, and swinging him upon his shoulder started for the schooner at a rapid run. He brought his prisoner in triumph, and stood him up on the deck where all could see him.

CHAPTER VI.

A SCAMP ON HIS DIGNITY.

THIS yere is the mean chap that done it all," continued the trapper. "Thar's none of us that'll ever see Frank ag'in. He's gone round on t'other side of the 'arth, an' some dark night, when he's sailin' along thinkin' of nothing, one of them big quids (the sailors had called the cuttle-fish 'squids') will rise outen the water all on a sudden, wrap his arms, two hundred feet long, all about the ship, an' that'll be the last of Frank. When be you goin' to hang this feller, cap'n ?"

Dick had an interested and anxious crowd of listeners. The officers of the schooner and the boys stood ranged in a circle in front of him, and behind were the sailors, who at first invaded the sacred precincts of the quarter-deck with much hesitation, holding their caps in their hands and momentarily expecting an order to retire ; but growing bolder by degrees, when they found that the captain, although he looked their way now and then, had nothing to say to them, they crowded up close behind the trapper, so that they could hear every word. There were also two other listeners—the men with the bludgeons, who had followed Dick Lewis in the hope of rescuing his prisoner. When these two worthies first came up, they acted as if they were about to board the vessel without ceremony ; but changed their minds when they saw half a dozen broad-shouldered seamen, in obedience to a sign from the officer of the deck, move up into the waist to receive them. The sailors, who had a pretty good idea of what had been going on, even before they had heard the trapper's story, would have been delighted to have the opportunity to toss these men ashore neck and heels; and the latter must have seen it in their countenances, for they backed away from the edge of the wharf and took up a position from which they could hear and see all that passed on the Stranger's deck.

Had Frank been as safe out of his troubles as Dick Lewis was, the boys would have been highly amused by the latter's description of the scenes through which he had passed ; but it was far from being a laughing matter now. Frank had been kidnapped ("shanghaied" the sailors called it) by the captain of the Tycoon or his agent, and there was no knowing what might become of him. Perhaps the hard fare and harder treatment he was certain to receive, might drive him to do something desperate. Uncle Dick Gaylord, however, was not troubled by any such misgivings. He knew that Frank possessed courage and prudence in no ordinary degree, and besides there were Lucas and Barton, the coxswain, on the same vessel. The former was an old whaleman, and the assistance he could render Frank in the way of teaching him his duties, might enable the boy to keep out of any very serious difficulties. But could he help him in any way ? That was the momentous question, and Uncle

Dick walked up and down his quarter-deck with his hands behind his back while he pondered upon it.

"Every word this man has uttered, as far as it concerns me and my doings, is false from head to tail," declared the bogus captain.

This was the first time he had spoken since he was brought on board the vessel. At first he was badly frightened, but while the trapper was telling his story, he had time to think over his situation and determine upon his line of defence.

"I dont know anything about this man and the other fellow he speaks of," he continued; "I never seen him before this morning, and I never tried to pass myself off as the captain of any ship."

Dick Lewis eyed him savagely while he was speaking, and when he ceased drew back his clenched hand. In a moment more the man would have measured his length on the deck, had not the captain interposed.

"Get ashore!" said he, shortly.

"O no, cap'n," replied the man, with an impudent smile. "This is a nice way you have of doing business, I do think! One of your friends commits an assault on me and drags me away from my peaceful home, and then you wash your hands of the matter by telling me to go ashore. That won't go down, by no means. Twenty dollars for damages will get rid of me, but not a cent less!"

"I can bring a dozen witnesses to prove that that man wasn't once outside of his house last night," said one of the ruffians on the dock. "I'm one of 'em, for I was with him all the evening and know everything he done."

"Rodgers!" exclaimed Uncle Dick.

"Here, sir," came the prompt response.

A stalwart sailor stepped quickly out from among his companions, and dashing his cap upon the deck stood behind the bogus captain pushing back his sleeves. A simple look from Uncle Dick would have sent the man flying over the schooner's side as if he had been thrown from a catapult.

"This is the last time I shall speak to you," continued Uncle Dick. "Get ashore!"

The bogus captain thought it best to obey, and

that too without a moment's hesitation. Once on the dock he was safe, and there he stopped long enough to say a parting word to Uncle Dick. "This matter will be settled in the court-room," said he, with a threatening shake of his head. "That man shall be arrested before he is an hour older."

With these words he walked off, followed by his companions. The boys looked first at him, then at the captain and finally at Dick Lewis, who stood the very picture of astonishment. "Why didn't you set the law a-goin'?" the trapper managed to ask at last.

"It would have been of no use," answered the master of the schooner. "Did't you hear what that man on the dock said? That indicated the defence they would bring up. We would find a court-room full of witnesses to prove an alibi—that is, that this man was somewhere else when the kidnapping was done."

"But it wouldn't be true, Uncle Dick," said Archie, who, like all the rest of the Club, invariably addressed the old sailor by this affectionate title. "If they swore to that, they would be guilty of perjury, and that is a state prison offence. Dick has told the truth."

"I know it. I am just as certain that everything he has described to us really happened, as I would be had I seen it all with my own eyes; but a justice would not take his unsupported word against that of a dozen men. And as for perjury, how would you fasten the crime upon these false witnesses that would be produced? If Frank, Lucas and Barton were here, we would have the game in our own hands; but they are miles away. This man knows we can prove nothing, and that is what makes him so impudent."

"I wish you had told Rodgers to throw him overboard, or else let Dick knock him down," said Eugene.

"And afterward had the satisfaction of paying a fine and costs," said the old sailor, with a laugh. "By the time your hair is as white as mine, Eugene, perhaps you will have learned something. I've got one fine to pay now."

"Why, how is that?" asked all the boys at once.

"Didn't you hear what that man said just as he went away? There'll be a policeman down here directly."

The boys looked toward the trapper. The expression of alarm which they had so often seen of late, had settled on his face again. He backed up against the rail for support, and looked wildly about as if he had half a mind to take to his heels. He stood more in fear of the law than he did of a grizzly bear. He had always thought that there was something wrong about it, and now he was firmly convinced of the fact. The law, as he understood it, was to restrain bad people, who were disposed to take advantage of their neighbors whenever an opportunity was offered; but he found that it was likely to prove a means of punishment to the innocent. It would have been just as impossible to give him a clear idea of its workings, as it would to make him understand the causes of the trade-winds or the theory of the ocean-currents.

"I've said a million times, an' Frank says that more'n a thousand, that I'd never put my old moccasins inside a city again, an' now I say it onct more an' I'll stick to it," said the trapper, solemnly, rais- ing his hand toward the masthead to give emphasis to his words. "I get skeared to death by cars an' steamboats, an' something's allers happenin'."

"Shoulder your rifle an' kit, Dick, an' let's be off," said old Bob, who up to this time had been a silent and amazed spectator and listener. "I'm afeared."

"So am I, Bob, but I dasen't. I dasen't go; the law will ketch me. I wish I was to the ole Bar's Hole, so't I could crawl in an' hide myself."

Dick leaned back against the rail again, rubbing his hands together and groaning as men sometimes do when they are sadly troubled in spirit. The boys tried hard to set his mind at rest. They assured him that no harm should come to him, for they and Uncle Dick were not only able but ready and willing to stand between him and all difficulties; but the trapper said he didn't want them to do it. If any- body was to go to jail (thrusting people into jail and hanging them Dick thought were the only punish-

ments in vogue in civilized communities) it should
be himself and nobody else. Furthermore, he did
not see why it was necessary that any one should be
called upon to stand between him and difficulty.
He had only been following out his natural impulses
in trying to bring the bogus captain to justice, and
now he must suffer for it. He shook his head, re-
fusing to be comforted, and showed a desire to be
alone with his own thoughts; so the boys left him
and turned to Uncle Dick, who was once more
pacing his quarter-deck, after holding a short consultation with his officers.

"I know what you want," said the old sailor, as
the boys approached him in a body. "You are
anxious to know what I am going to do for Frank.
I can only guess at the best plan, and follow it out
to the best of my judgment. What do you think
ought to be done?"

The boys had no suggestions to offer. One thing
was certain, and that was that Frank would not long
submit to harsh treatment. A young man who had
commanded a fine vessel in Uncle Sam's navy would

not consent to take rank next below the captain's
dog, as the sailors in the Tycoon's forecastle had
assured him he would do as long as he remained in
that ship. If the opportunity were ever offered, he
would lay his case before the consul of the first port
at which the vessel touched; and failing that he
would probably be driven to desert. In either case
the boys did not expect to see him again. If the
consul protected him, he would be sent to the
nearest port in the United States free of expense,
and he had money enough in his pocket—about
twenty dollars, Archie thought—to support him
until he could receive a remittance from home. If
he was compelled to desert he would probably ship
on the first vessel he could find, just as Chase had
done, and she might take him to the remotest corner
of the earth. All this would sadly interfere with
the Club's arrangements. They thought as much
of Frank as his cousin did—so much that they one
and all declared that they did not care to continue
their voyage without him. They couldn't enjoy
themselves, for they would worry about him all the

while, and if they were to be separated from him they would rather go home and stay there. If their pleasant party and their cruise were to be broken up, they had the boarding-house keeper to thank for it, and Walter declared that there was no punishment known to the law half severe enough for him.

Uncle Dick listened while the boys were talking, and said he fully agreed with them. "Even if Frank should succeed in escaping from the Tycoon, and had a vessel at his command or money enough to take him just where he wanted to go, he would not know which way to steer to find us," said he, "for you boys will remember that you did not decide upon anything definite, and Frank doesn't know whether we are going to Alaska or Japan."

"And all through my foolishness," said Eugene, bitterly. "I wish I had given up, and gone where the others wanted to go."

"So do I," said Bab.

"Don't reproach yourselves," replied Uncle Dick. "You had plenty of sport during your debates, and you were not supposed to know that such an emergency as this was about to arise. But perhaps we can do something by following the Tycoon."

"Yes, if we only knew where she is going."

"I have an idea that I do know. She is bound for the Japan station, so the sailors in her forecastle told Dick Lewis. Well, now, she is short-handed. She must be, for her mate released Dick from his irons and brought him on deck to help make sail. She'll never go on her station without a full crew, and the nearest place at which she can get it is the Sandwich Islands. There she will undoubtedly ship Kanakas enough to make up her complement. Then she'll go out for a three or four months' cruise, and come back and fit out for the Japan station. Now, if we can reach Honolulu before she leaves, we shall probably be able to effect the release of our men. If it were not for this incident that has just happened I would sail at once."

"Why can't you do it any way?" asked Walter, who did not like to waste even a moment.

"Because we must see Lewis out of his trouble. If he goes ashore without some one to protect him, he will be sure to fall into the hands of those sharpers, who will frighten him out of the last article of value he's got."

"Cap'n," said Dick, suddenly, "will you take us with you—me and Bob?"

The old sailor looked in astonishment, and so did the boys.

"I'm afeared to go ashore," continued the trapper, who had been holding a council of war with his chum, "an' so is Bob. 'Sides it's a thing we never done yet—run off an' leave Frank in trouble, an' we've knowed him too long to do it now!"

"My good fellow," said Uncle Dick, with a smile, "if Frank were lost in the woods, you and Bob would be just the men to assist him; but you can't help him in any way now."

"Mebbe we can, cap'n. An' even if we can't, we don't want to go back hum without knowing what's come on him. We shouldn't see no peace of mind."

Uncle Dick did not speak for several minutes. He knew just how much these rude men thought of Frank, and told himself that their desire to see him safe among friends again before they took leave of him for ever, was perfectly natural; but there were the dangers they expected to meet on the "under side of the earth"—the Flying Dutchman, the whales, the monstrous "quids"—could they stand all these? "Lewis," said he, suddenly, "have you and your companion fully made up your minds on this point?"

"Yes, an' we won't never change 'em nuther. We allers stand to what we say."

"That settles the matter. Mr. Baldwin, while I am gone to the custom house, hail the first tug you see and stand by to get under way."

The boys would have been delighted by this arrangement a few hours before, but their feelings were different now. They had something to think of besides the amusement they expected the trappers to furnish them.

Uncle Dick went ashore and walked rapidly away, leaving the boys to themselves. Although they were impatient to be off, the time did not hang heav-

8

ily on their hands, for they had much to talk about. They fully expected the trappers to change their minds when they saw the preparations that were being made for getting under way, but Dick and Bob were not that sort. There was a dogged expression on their faces, such as might have been seen there had the backwoodsmen been in the power of savage foes who were making ready to torture them at the stake. It said that they fully realized the dangers before them, and were prepared to meet them like men who had never shown the white feather.

"Now, if Frank were only here, and if Dick and Bob would get rid of some of their foolish notions, we could look forward to some fun, couldn't we?" siad Eugene.

"*If* and *if!*" said Walter. "It is surprising how often that little word stands in our way."

"I have been thinking that Dick's short sojourn on the Tycoon has made matters worse for Frank than they would otherwise have been," said Bab, anxiously. "The three principal officers have felt the weight of his arm, and of course they'll have to take satisfaction out of somebody."

"Dick," said Archie, suddenly, "why don't you encourage us by saying that Frank will be sure to come out all right? That's what you used to tell us whenever he got into trouble."

"But he was on the prairie then, an' now he's among civilized folks," replied the trapper.

"Which means, I suppose, that this is the worst scrape he ever got into."

Dick nodded his head.

"I don't know about that," said George Le Dell. "I think if he had his choice, he would rather be where he is now than in the prison at Shreveport, if he had to go through what he did when he made his escape. Frank has been in some tight places, but somehow he has always managed to squeeze through without much trouble."

"And he never was hurt that I remember, except when he burned that house in which Colonel Harrison made his headquarters," said Archie.

"When *you* burned it, you mean," said George.

" *You* did that, and if you had been a line instead of a staff officer, you would have got another stripe around your arm for it, too.   I told the Colonel all about it after you left our house."

"Why did you do that?" exclaimed Archie, hastily.   "Now I shall never dare to meet him again."

"Ha! ha!" laughed George.   "Why, he is one of your warmest friends.   I told him because I wanted him to know that the boy who killed that bear and beat Somers in a fair race through the woods, had something in him.   The Colonel scolded me for not telling him before.   He said if he had known it while you were in our neighborhood, you wouldn't have got away from his house for one good long month at least.   He would have kept you if he'd had to put a guard over you."

" Well, I shouldn't have enjoyed the visit."

" You couldn't have helped yourself, if plenty of hunting, riding and good company are aids to enjoyment."

From this subject the boys gradually got back to

the one that occupied the most of their minds and
thoughts, and that was Frank's sudden disap-
pearance. They asked the trapper a multitude of
questions, but learned nothing new, for he had
already told his story in detail. While they were
talking Uncle Dick returned, and the tug being
alongside and the pilot aboard, the lines were cast
off and the Stranger swung slowly around until her
bow pointed toward the headlands at the entrance
to the bay. In the bustle and hurry that followed
the boys found time to turn an eye toward the trappers now and then, but they saw no signs of regret
or alarm on their faces; and when the lines that
held the tug were let go, and the steamer with a
farewell shriek of her whistle turned back toward
the city, and the schooner unfolded her white wings
one after the other, and the Golden Gate was passed,
and the broad expanse of the Pacific was fairly
spread out before them, there were still no signs of
backing out. But it was too late now. The die
was cast, and Dick and old Bob were bound for the
" under side of the earth !"

CHAPTER VII.

TOO LATE.

THE very presence of Uncle Dick was enough to infuse new life and comfort into the boys, who were disposed to make themselves miserable over the absence of their genial companion. The old sailor believed in looking on the bright side of things, and thought there was no use in worrying over the matter that they could not just then better in any way. His example made a great change in the feelings of the Club.

"Now, Walter," said he, briskly, "we are fairly afloat again, and our sailing-master having deserted us, we are compelled to call on you to fill his place. Suppose you work out a course for us. We're bound for the Sandwich Islands, Eugene; which way are they from here?"

"Oh, you can't catch me on that," replied the boy, "for I posted myself only a few days ago. The twentieth parallel runs through them. They're in the same latitude as Vera Cruz, in Mexico."

"Well, I want to make the run in as short a time as may be, so what shall I do?"

"Stand to the southwest to get the benefit of the northeast trades, and the equatorial current. The same route would take you to China or Japan."

"Suppose, now, we were in China and wanted to come back to the States: would I follow the same course?"

"No, sir. You would steer in a northerly direction until you got between the parellels of thirty-five and forty-five degrees north latitude, and there you would find strong westerly winds to help you along. Perhaps you'd get some assistance from the North Pacific drift current, but on that point I am not sure."

"Well, it is just as well you are not," shouted Walter from the cabin, where he was busy with his chart. "The North Pacific drift current might help you if you wanted to go to Alaska from China. When it strikes the shores of our continent it divides, part of it flowing on down the coast and forming the California coast current, and the rest bending back across the Pacific again; so it would retard your progress rather than help you."

"Well, I am not the sailing-master of this craft, am I?" replied Eugene. "If I was, I'd keep posted. Besides, almost anybody with a chart before him, could clatter away as though his tongue was hung in the middle. Wait till Frank gets back if you want to talk about navigation."

"He's a good one, that's a fact," said Uncle Dick. "He's as fit to command a vessel as I am."

Just then Walter came up, having worked out a course, which being approved by the captain and given to the officer of the deck, the bow of the Stranger was brought around a point or two, and the voyage was fairly begun. There was nothing to be done now, but to await developments with all the patience they possessed.

But few incidents worthy of record happened

during the voyage, which, after they struck the
trade winds became monotonous enough. The
schooner bowled along before a fine breeze, and as
it was never necessary to change the sails, there
was no work to be done except ordinary ship's duty.
The Club passed the time mostly in reading and
conversation with the trappers, who, as soon as they
fully recovered from their sea-sickness, kept a constant lookout for some of those terrible dangers
which had been so graphically described to them.
By dint of much talking and argument the boys
finally succeeded in making them take a more sensi-
ble view of their situation, and as the days wore
away without bringing with them any of the perils
they had expected to encounter, the backwoodsmen
began to act a little more like themselves. But
when an ignorant person once gets hold of an idea
it is almost impossible to make him let go of it, and
the trappers' minds could not be set wholly at rest.
They steadily refused to go into the forecastle at
night, and always slept on deck. The boys found
the reason for this in a remark they heard Bob

make to his companion. They wanted plenty of elbow room when they reached the under side of the earth, the old fellow said, so that when the schooner dropped off among the clouds, they could take to the water. They saw sharks, dolphins and flying-fish (the trappers began to put more faith in what the boys said after they had seen one of the latter rise from the water and sail through the air like a bird on the wing), and one day the sailors pointed out to them an object which made them believe that their time had come. It first showed itself while the boys were at dinner. They were summoned on deck by the officers of the watch, and found themselves close alongside the first whale they had ever seen. The monster was taking matters very leis-urely, moving along about a hundred yards from the schooner, lifting his huge head out of the water now and then and spouting a cloud of spray into the air, and although the vessel was running at a rate of eight miles an hour, he kept pace with her without the least exertion. The boys were all dis-appointed.

" This must be a small one," said George.

" Small !" echoed Uncle Dick. " How big do you think a whale is, any how—as big as the Rocky Mountains ?"

" No, sir; but I have read that they have been found sixty and seventy feet long," replied George.

" Well, this fellow is every inch of eighty, and I shouldn't wonder if he was ninety feet in length."

" I wish some whaler would come along and pitch into him," said Eugene. " I'd like to see the operation of catching a whale."

" If fifty whalers should come along they would not trouble this fellow," said Uncle Dick.

" Why not ?"

" Because he is neither a sperm nor a right whale. He belongs to the species known as finbacks. He would not yield oil or bone enough to pay for the trouble of lowering the boats, and besides he is so swift and strong that it would be dangerous to meddle with him."

The finback kept alongside the schooner for nearly a mile, and during that time the boys had

ample opportunity to take a good view of him. He
sank and rose at regular intervals, executing the
manœuvre with an ease and grace that was astonishing, and now and then he showed so much of his
huge bulk above the water that the boys opened
their eyes in amazement, and Featherweight declared that there was no end to him. The longer
they looked at him the larger he seemed to grow.
At length he began to edge away from the schooner,
and finally disappeared. Then each boy turned
and looked at his neighbor to see what he thought
about it.

"What makes you look so sober?" demanded
Featherweight of Archie, who stood by pulling his
chin, and gazing fixedly at the spot where the whale
had last been seen.

"I was just thinking," was the reply.

"And I'll warrant we can all tell what you were
thinking about," said George. "I guess there is
no one in this small party who would like to be
ordered into a small boat to attack a beast of that
size, and you were wondering what Frank's feelings

will be the first time he tries it. Well, I don't want to know them by experience."

Archie walked to the side and looked over into the water, while George turned to Dick and Bob, who just then came up. Their faces were very white.

" Well, Dick," said George, " you have seen your first whale, and it isn't such a terrible looking object after all, is it ?"

" I dunno," replied the trapper. " If the babies look like that, what must the ole ones be ?"

" The babies ?" repeated George.

" One of the fellows showed that thing to me when it fust come in sight, and I showed it to Rodgers, but he couldn't see it. Rodgers, he called another of the sailors, and he said he could see something, but it was so small he couldn't tell whether it was a whale or not."

" Now, Dick, don't you believe a word those men in the forecastle say to you," said Eugene, indignantly. " Uncle Dick says that is one of the largest whales he ever saw."

" Wal, Rodgers he couldn't see it at fust 'cause it was so small, but when he *did* see it, he said mebbee it was a baby. He said the ole one will be along purty soon lookin' fur it, an' then we'll see a whale. If the ole one don't find the baby, she'll think we've done something to it, an' she'll brush us off'n the 'arth like a feller would brush a fly off his Sundy trowsers."

The trappers were frightened again, and for the rest of the day kept close company with their young friends, no doubt feeling safer in their presence than anywhere else. The boys, one and all, exerted themselves to correct the wrong impressions they had received, but the foremast hands had had the first chance at them, as Fred remarked, and it was a matter of impossibility to set their fears at rest. For a week afterward Dick and his companion kept a sharp lookout, expecting every minute to see the old whale coming in search of her young one; but she did not appear, and the next thing that happened to relieve the monotony of the voyage, was the discovery of land, dead ahead. Walter had been anxiously looking for it for the last twenty-four hours. Having taken Frank's place as sailing-master, he was eager to earn a reputation as a navigator, and he was not a little elated to find that he had made no mistake.

The discovery of land set the sailors going again. Rodgers and a few of his companions, who, when the trappers were in hearing, were continually talking about mermaids and dragons and other sea monsters, and the awful sights that would be presented when they came to the under side of the earth, looked through their hands at the dim outline in advance, and after comparing notes in a tone of voice loud enough for Dick and Bob to hear, declared that it wasn't land after all—that the man at the mast was mistaken.

"That's no more land nor I be," declared Rodgers. "If my head is worth a tar-bucket, it is the old whale. She can't find her baby, and so she's coming down to ask the skipper what he's done with it. She's coming like lightning too. Can't

you see the water a boiling up under her bows? I
can."

"Now, mate, I think it's a squid," said another,
"and he's waiting there to gobble up something.
I can see his long arms resting on the water, and
ready to catch the first moving thing that comes
within reach. I hope the cap'n 'll keep away a few
points."

"Mebbe he don't know what it is," said a third,
"and I think Lewis had better go aft and tell him
about it—I do indeed!"

"'Taint a whale nor a squid neither," said an old
gray-headed seaman, who, using his hands for a
spy-glass, had been looking at the island ever since
they first came in sight of it. "It's the equator.
I can see the waves rolling over it!"

"Well, Jack, you've been to sea longer nor me and
ought to know about these things," said Rodgers.
"I seen the waves, but I thought they was the bone
the whale was carrying in her teeth. When we get
over it, if we ever do, we're on the under side of the
earth, ain't we?"

" That's what's the matter," said the gray-headed sailor.

Dick fairly jumped, as each one of these opinions was solemnly advanced, and hurried off to speak to the boys. The latter, especially Eugene and Archie, could hardly refrain from laughing outright at his ludicrous display of terror, but they quieted his fears as well as they could, and by giving him a solemn promise that they would see him safely through any danger that might arise if he would remain close by them, they succeeded in keeping him out of the company of the foremast hands all the rest of the day. But it was not until nearly sunset that the fears the sailors had conjured up were entirely banished. By that time the object that had excited his alarm was so plainly visible that Dick could see for himself that it was land and nothing else.

The boys did not see many of the new and novel sights that were presented to their gaze, as the Stranger made her way through the strait that runs between the islands of Hawaii and Mani. They

9

had eyes for nothing but the whale ship they expected to find there. The huge fishing canoes they
saw the next day; the natives that came aboard
in swarms while they were running about in the
light, baffling winds they found under the lee of the
land, the fruits they offered for barter—none of
these things possessed the interest for them that
they would under almost any other circumstances.
They paid little attention to anything but the vessels that now and then passed them. But the Tycoon
was not among them.

Uncle Dick took time, as he passed along, to look
into every bay and inlet where the Tycoon was likely
to be, and it was not until nearly a week after they
first sighted the Sandwich Islands that the Stranger
dropped anchor outside the coral reef that marks the
entrance to the harbor of Honolulu. As the wind
came strong down the mountain gorges, everything
was made snug, and then the gig was called away
and the captain set out for the town, leaving the
boys to enjoy themselves as best they could during
his absence. But it was dull business, this trying

to pass away the time when they were so impatient and anxious. They kept up their spirits by telling one another that something would surely happen to restore their friend Frank to them, but the face that Uncle Dick brought back with him, when he returned six hours later, dashed all their hopes to the ground. No sooner was the gig fairly hoisted at the davits, than he gave the order to heave up the anchor and go to sea. The boys stood around and looked at one another in silence while these orders were being executed, and when Uncle Dick went into the cabin, they followed him.

"Too late, boys," said he.

"Has the Tycoon been here?" asked Walter.

"Yes; she has done just what I thought she would do. She shipped a crew of natives and has gone out for a three months' cruise. When that is ended she will come back and fit out for Japan."

"And what about Frank?"

"Haven't heard a word of him. The consul saw only the captain, and he was here just long enough to ship his crew. We missed our object by just three days."

"I don't understand how we missed it at all," said Eugene. "We certainly lost no time."

"But you must remember that the Tycoon is a large ship, and that she probably carries as much canvas in her courses and spanker as we can spread on all our masts and yards. We can't expect to sail with her."

"What are we going to do now?" asked Bab.

"We are going to see if we can find her. It will be almost like searching for a needle in a haystack, but we don't want to remain here idle for three months."

"Of course not," said Eugene, quickly. "That would never do. While we are moving about we shall feel that we are doing something for Frank, even if we don't find him."

"Exactly," said Uncle Dick.

"What will you do if we find the Tycoon?" inquired Walter.

"I shall probably be able to present the matter

to her captain in such a way that he will be willing to release Frank and make him some amends for what he has done—I *think* I shall be able to do so," said the old sailor, with a look in his eye that spoke volumes. "But if I should fail, he will be arrested as soon as he comes back here."

This was all Uncle Dick had to say, and it afforded the boys very little satisfaction. They had confidently expected that Frank would be restored to them when they reached the Sandwich Islands, and this was a sore disappointment. Where was he now? Where was he while the Tycoon was lying in the harbor of Honolulu? What was the reason he had not done as he advised the deserter to do—insisted on seeing the American consul? The boys could only speculate upon these points, and they had ample leisure to do it—almost six weeks. During that time every ship they could come up with was spoken, but the Tycoon was not among them, and neither could they gain any information concerning her. The boys were getting discouraged and very down-hearted, and had it not been for Uncle Dick there is no telling how they would have lived through it.

One night the officer of the deck reported that there was a whaler a few miles distant "trying out"—that is, rendering out the oil of a whale she had recently captured. The Stranger's bow was at once pointed toward her, and at sunrise the two vessels were within speaking distance.

" Now just listen to me a minute and I'll tell you what's a fact," said Perk, who with the rest of the Club stood in the waist, attentively regarding the ship as she came toward them carrying a huge bone in her teeth, "there's something about that craft that looks familiar."

" I was just thinking so myself," said Eugene.

He glanced toward Uncle Dick, who, during the last quarter of an hour had kept his glass levelled at the ship, and edged away toward the officer of the deck. " It can't be that that is the vessel we're looking for, is it, Mr. Baldwin?" said he.

" If it isn't her, it's her sister," replied the officer, with some excitement.

Before Eugene could carry this news to his companions the ship backed her main topsail, and as Uncle Dick, with an exclamation of astonishment that had a good deal of meaning in it, seized his trumpet, her captain appeared upon her bulwarks. The boys, through their glasses, had a plain view of him, and the general verdict was that he was a rough-looking fellow—one who, judging by his appearance, was capable of almost anything.

"It is the same man we saw in the whale-boat," declared Eugene, his voice rendered husky by excitement. "I know him, even if he hasn't got his gray suit on."

"I confess that I can't see any resemblance," said Bab, taking his glass down from his eyes long enough to bring it to a better focus.

It would have required a person with a very lively imagination to recognise anybody at that distance, especially in such clothes as those in which the captain was dressed. He wore a tarpaulin on his head, a red shirt open at the throat, and a pair of coarse trowsers, which were thrust into the tops of heavy sea boots; and as some of these articles had been made for larger, and others for smaller men than himself, they fitted him oddly enough.

"Ship ahoy!" roared Uncle Dick.

"Ay, ay, sir!" shouted the captain of the whaler.

"What ship is that?" asked Uncle Dick.

The answer was given in a loud tone of voice, but the words were indistinct. The captain talked as if he had a mouthful of something. The only part of the reply that the Stranger's crew understood was that the ship was seventeen months out of Nantucket, and that she had nine hundred barrels of oil in the hold.

"What does he say is the name of his ship, Mr. Baldwin?" asked Uncle Dick.

"I understood him to say Eli Coon, sir," said the officer.

"That sounds wonderfully like Tycoon, doesn't it?" whispered George.

"And what does he call himself, Mr. Baldwin?" continued Uncle Dick.

" Captain Hank Wilson, were the words I caught, sir.":

" What schooner is that ?" shouted the captain of the whaler.

" The Stranger, Captain Richard Gaylord, just out of Honolulu," answered Uncle Dick ; and the words were so plain and distinct that the master of the whaler could have heard them if he had been twice as far away.

" I'll send a boat aboard of you."

" Very good, sir," replied Uncle Dick. " There is something strange about this, Mr. Baldwin," he added. " That is the Tycoon if I ever saw her, but that isn't the scoundrel who commanded her while she was in the harbor of San Francisco. Stand by, now, and if any of our men come off in his boat we'll see that they don't go back."

There was no confusion on board the Stranger— there never was, for the discipline was too perfect for that—but everybody was highly excited. And the excitement was increased when the second mate went forward with the order, which he gave in a low voice : "All hands stand by, and be ready to jump when you hear the word." The sailors knew what that meant, and while some pushed back their sleeves, others laid handspikes where they could find them again at a moment's warning ; and having thus prepared for any emergency, they moved to the side in a body, and awaited the coming of the whaler's boat with no little impatience. She came in sight at length, rounding the stern of the ship. Presently one of the men whispered something, which was passed along from one to another, until it reached the ears of the boys in the waist :

"I see Lucas in that boat, and Barton too !"

"But where is Frank ?" said Archie, anxiously. "If he is aboard that ship now is his time to jump overboard and swim out to us."

"Look at Dick Lewis," whispered Bab, suddenly.

The boys with one accord turned their eyes toward the trapper. He stood on the forecastle with his hands on the rail, over which he was leaning as far as he could without losing his balance, and his

eyes were fastened upon the approaching boat with
a gaze such as a hawk might bestow upon the prey
it was about to seize. As the boat aproached nearer
and veered round to come alongside, Dick gradually drew back out of sight and walked toward the
stern to meet her.

"If that is the captain of the Tycoon standing
in the stern of that boat," said Archie, "he will be
a well-thumped man before he gets fairly on deck,
unless Uncle Dick interferes in time."

"It isn't he," said Eugene. "I was mistaken.
But he's a hard-looking customer all the same."

The boat came nearer with every stroke of its
crew, but the boys could not see any one in it whom
they recognised. The backs of the oarsmen were
turned toward them, and the captain kept his tarpaulin drawn low over his forehead, while the wind
had turned the collar of his shirt up about his ears,
so that his face was most effectually concealed.

With a few strokes more the boat was alongside,
and the red-shirted captain's head appeared above
the Stranger's rail. Then Dick began to bestir

himself.   With a bound like a tiger he sprang forward and grasped the captain by the shoulders.

"Avast there, Lewis!" roared Uncle Dick. "What are you about? If you attempt any violence I'll throw you over to the whales!"

"No, I reckon not," replied the trapper. "This feller can't fool ole Dick Lewis, no matter what sort o' clothes he's got onto him!"

As he said this he dragged the captain bodily over the rail, and lifting him in his arms as he would an infant, carried him toward the quarter-deck.

CHAPTER VIII.

GENTLEMAN BLACK.

G O on deck now, and let me give you fair warning that if you don't behave yourselves you'll
go overboard before you can think twice!"

It was the mate of the Tycoon who spoke, and
who gave this order to Frank and the three sailors
in the forecastle, after he had released them from
their irons. The officer did not look much as he did
the last time Frank saw him. He wore a handkerchief about his head and over his left eye, but it did
not wholly conceal his face, which was badly swollen
and discolored. He was in a fair way to remember
his meeting with the trapper for some time to come.

During the hour that Frank was confined in the
forecastle his mind was exceedingly busy. His
companions in trouble civilly answered all the

questions he asked them, but did not seem inclined
to talk, so Frank had opportunity to think over his
situation and try to determine upon some course of
action.   The first thing he did was to congratulate
himself on the fact that none of his companions
were with him on the Tycoon.   Had Walter, Bab,
Archie or any of the rest gone ashore with him
when he went after his rifle, they would now have
been in the same predicament as himself; and
according to Frank's way of thinking that would
have been a calamity indeed.   He expected to suffer—his mind was fully made up to that,—but he
was strong and healthy and better able to endure
hardship than any of the young friends he had left
on board the Stranger.   He had no fears for
Dick Lewis.   The trapper was as tough as a pine
knot—nothing seemed to make any impression on
him—and if he could only be induced to keep his
temper under control, and pay no attention to the
blows and insults he was sure to receive, he would
get on well enough.   Still he thought more of him
than he did of Lucas and Barton, who were sleeping

soundly in their bunk. These two were old sailors and could stand anything. They were not likely to have as easy times as they had had on board the Stranger, but they were accustomed to hard work and hard treatment, and when safe off the Tycoon they would have another story to help while away the lonely hours of the mid watch.

Thus it will be seen that Frank was disposed to make the best of his misfortunes, and to look on the bright side of things. But there was one fact that troubled him not a little, and that was, his connection with the Club was severed. He did not expect to see any of its members again, not even Archie, for years to come. He would be released from the Tycoon some day—just as soon as he could gain the ear of some American consul for a moment—but he would not know which way to turn to find the Stranger, and so would have nothing left him but to make the best of his way back to Lawrence. That would be a great disappointment to him. He had anticipated much pleasure from his vist to foreign countries, and it was hard to abandon the voyage, just as his expectations were about to be realized, and go back to the monotonous, hum-drum routine of village life. But as there was no help for it, it was useless to repine, Frank told himself. He would do his duty as well as he could while he remained on board the Tycoon, but he was under no obligations to stay with her any longer than he was compelled to do so; and the first time she dropped anchor in port there would be one of her crew missing, unless the officers took the precaution to deprive him of his liberty.

While Frank was meditating in this way the mate came into the forecastle, and after taking off his irons, ordered him on deck. Ascending the ladder he found a small crew engaged in setting things to rights. The third mate, who met him as he came up, put him to work with the rest, and for the next hour Frank was kept so busy that he did not have time to see much of his surroundings. He took a look around now and then for Dick Lewis, and wondered what sort of work the clumsy trapper would make in doing sailor's duty.

" Was you looking for your pardner, sir ?" asked a seaman who was busy at his side. (The " sir" came out almost involuntarily, as if the man instinctively felt that Frank was in some way entitled to that show of respect.)

" Yes ; I was looking for that tall, broad-shouldered man in buckskin who came aboard with me."

" Well, sir, he's gone !"

" Gone ! Where ?"

" I don't know, for he can't be found alow nor aloft. He must have jumped overboard."

" O, I hope not !" said Frank anxiously.

" If he has, it is all right, sir, because he'd a done it sooner or later. I'll not stay aboard here much longer, unless there's a great change for the better. Things couldn't be worse."

" Don't do anything desperate," said Frank. " It won't pay. But what made this man of whom we were speaking jump overboard ?"

" I don't know, sir. I was busy when he came up. The first thing I knew there was a rumpus ; the cap'n and two of the mates were laid out as

10

flat as slap-jacks, and the man hasn't been seen since."

"Were we far from shore?"

"Only about three or four miles."

"O, then it is all right. Dick is safe. He can swim double that distance."

"Well, I can't; but I wish I could have gone with him. I've seen two men go overboard since I've been on this craft, and if I was with 'em now among the sharks, my troubles would all be over."

Here was direct confirmation of the story the deserter had told on board the Stranger. Frank drew a long breath, and from that moment a settled determination took possession of him.

The work was all done at last, the watches told off and one of them ordered below. The one to which Frank belonged remained on deck to handle the ship, which was making long boards to gain an offing. Two or three times every hour they were called upon to trim the sails as the ship changed her course and stood off on another tack, and the rest of the time the crew lounged about the windlass. But there was none of that story-telling in which the crew of the Stranger engaged on such occasions, to make the time hang less heavily on their hands. The men sat sullen and silent, and as they were no company for Frank, he strolled aft to make an inspection of the craft which was likely to be his home for long weeks and perhaps months to come. She was different from other ships he had seen only in the number of boats she carried at her davits, and in her try-works, which were fitted up amidships. These were built of masonry, contained three large kettles, and were so constructed that a body of water could be kept under the furnace to prevent the fire from burning the deck.

Having seen all he cared to see, Frank went forward again, and leaning over the windlass thought of the friends he was fast leaving behind him and of the trapper. He hoped from the bottom of his heart that Dick had jumped overboard. If such was the case he had saved himself many an hour of suffering, and had placed himself in no danger. It was but a short distance to the shore for such a swimmer as he knew the trapper to be, and besides there were vessels constantly passing in and out of the harbor, so that on a calm night like that he had only to call for help to get it. The trapper had learned enough from the three men in the forecastle, if he could only remember it, to put Uncle Dick Gaylord on the track of the Tycoon, and perhaps matters might not turn out so badly after all. If the Stranger followed the Tycoon to Japan, his release would certainly be effected; but how would he fare in the meantime? He wished that some discontented boy who had read yellow-covered novels until he had become thoroughly disgusted with home and all its surroundings, and sighed for the wild, free, romantic life of a sailor, could be in his place just then.

A short time before Frank's watch on deck was ended, he heard a rustling in one of the bunks below, and looking into the forecastle saw that the boatswain's mate, having come to his senses, was sitting up and staring about him in great bewilderment. The old-sea dog did not know where he was, but he quickly became aware that he was aboard some craft that was in motion, and catching up his cap he sprang out of his bunk and ran up the ladder. At the top he found Frank, whom he recognised at once.

"Where are we, cap'n?" he exclaimed; "and how long have we been under way?"

The sailors belonging to the Stranger's crew were pretty well acquainted with the history of their captain and his passengers. They conceived a great respect for Frank when they learned that he had been all through the late war, and that he had, by his own unaided efforts, worked his way from the forecastle to the quarter-deck, and falling into Uncle Dick's habit, they invariably addressed him by his old naval title, and were as careful to salute him whenever they passed him as they were to salute their commander.

Before Frank had time to reply, the boatswain's mate had glanced about the deck of the whaler, and some faint suspicions seemed to creep into his mind. "This ain't the Stranger, cap'n!" said he.

"Who are you talking to?" demanded the first mate, who just then came forward.

"I was speaking to Cap'n Nelson, sir," was the reply.

"Who is he? Where is he?" asked the mate, roughly.

"There he stands, sir."

"Well, you just drop all that," said the officer, who was plainly very much surprised, "and hereafter bear in mind that there is only one captain aboard this ship and only one first mate. Get on deck, here. You belong to this watch!"

"Ay, ay, sir," replied Lucas. "Now here's a lubberly go, cap'n," he added in a low tone, as the mate went aft out of earshot.

"Be careful," said Frank, quickly. "Remember the mate's order and drop that title and all others when you speak to me. Just recollect that I occupy a lower position aboard this craft than you do, for you are an able seaman and I am not."

"But what craft is this and what's happened us?"

asked the boatswain's mate, earnestly—"shang-haied?"

"Yes, and this ship is the Tycoon."

"I knew it," said the old sailor, striking his open palm with his clenched hand. "Serves me right."

"I don't know how you came here. Perhaps you can tell."

"I took a drink, sir," said Lucas, hanging his head.

"Ah! yes; and you didn't get it out of the scuttle-butt either, did you? Pure water would not have robbed you of your senses."

Then Frank went on to tell of his meeting with the bogus captain and the manner in which he and the trapper had been enticed on board the whaler. The old sailor was greatly distressed to know that it was through him that Frank had been brought into trouble. He offered to make amends by jumping overboard, and seemed to be hurt because Frank would not consent to it. While he was trying to comfort the mate the watch was called and Frank and the rest ordered below.

Thus far things seemed to be working as well as could be expected under the circumstances. Frank had heard a few hard words from the officers, but he had seen no blows struck. This, however, was only the calm that preceded the storm. The next morning the captain made his appearance on deck, just as the crew were ordered to turn to, and then the trouble began. Frank recognised him at once, for he wore the same clothes he had on when he passed the Stranger in the whale-boat. He proved to be quite as brutal as he looked, and a constitutional grumbler. He found fault with everything. Nothing could be done to suit him. He swore at the officers, and they in turn swore at the men, and struck right and left with whatever came first to their hands—that is, the first and second mates did. The third mate, whom Frank had heard addressed as Mr. Gale, took no part in the swearing and striking. He did not speak to the men as if they were dogs, but his orders were just as emphatic, just as readily understood and quite as promptly obeyed. Frank took a liking to the man

at once. Like himself, he seemed very much out
of place on board the Tycoon.

The captain was anxious to get his small crew
into shape for work before he reached the fishing-
grounds, and almost the first thing he did was to
order out a "dummy whale," which was a spar
towed over the stern. Then the boats' crews were
selected. There proved to be enough to man two
boats, leaving a sufficient number of the crew on
board to act as ship-keepers. Frank and Lucas were
assigned to the captain's boat, the former being
seated at the bow oar. This was a position of
responsibility, as Frank very soon learned. A
whale when struck by a harpoon sometimes starts
to run; and in such a case it is the duty of the bow
oar to seize the line, draw the boat up alongside
the whale, and hold it there while the captain uses
his lance.

Everything being in readiness, the boats were
lowered, and for the next three hours were manœu-
vred about the spar, until it seemed to Frank that
the inside of his hands was all in a blaze. To make

matters worse, the captain swore at him for his awkwardness, and took him to task for answering "Very good, sir!" in response to an order, when he should have said "Ay, ay, sir!"   An officer in the navy is required to answer "Very good, sir," when receiving a command from a superior, to show that he understands it; but Frank was not in the navy now, and neither was he an officer.   He was a foremast hand on board a whaler, occupying a position a good deal lower than the captain's dog, he began to think.

The boats were finally ordered back to the ship, and after they had been hoisted at the davits, the falls laid down in Flemish coil on deck, and the spar hauled aboard, Frank heard the order passed—

"Send that gentleman in the black suit aft here."

Frank knew in a moment that he was the one designated.   He claimed to be a gentleman and he wore a suit of black clothes—he was the only one on board who did—so he promptly answered to the summons.   "Here, sir," said he.

When he reached the quarter-deck he removed his hat and waited for the captain to speak to him.

" So you know your name, do you?" exclaimed the skipper, gruffly.

"My name is Nelson, sir."

"But it suits me to call you Gentleman Black."

"Very—ay, ay, sir," replied Frank, who knew that he was expected to say something.

" Shoulder that handspike," continued the captain, pointing out the implement, "and march up and down the deck like a soger as you are. Carry it until you learn not to say 'very good' to me. What business is it of yours whether my orders are very good or very bad? I'll soon take them airs out of you."

Frank picked up the handspike, and placing it on his shoulder, began walking up and down the deck like a sentry on his beat. A landsman would have seen no significance in this punishment, but the sailors did, and the boatswain's mate and the coxswain (the latter had recovered his senses and gone to work with the rest) were highly indignant. A seaman regards it as an insult to be called a soldier. It implies that he is a "skulker"—that he shirks his duty.

This was the second time that Frank had been punished on board ship. His first offence, as we know, was committed while he was in the navy, on board the receiving ship. He spilled some water on deck, and was obliged to wipe it up and carry a swab about the vessel until he saw some one else doing the same thing. He might have carried that swab all day, had not Archie taken pity on him and effected his release. His jolly little cousin was not at hand to help him now. Frank was glad that he was far away, and in no danger of ever being placed in a situation like his own.

Frank found that even a handspike grows heavy after a while, and when he had carried it four long hours, he would have been glad to put it down and rest; but his release did not come until his watch was called at twelve o'clock that night. From noon until midnight he paced the deck without a moment's pause, a bite to eat or a drop to drink. He was tired and sleepy, but was obliged to remain on deck four hours longer, or until the watch to which he belonged was ordered below. It was pretty hard, Frank told himself, and provoking, too, to find somebody ready to make sport of him, as one of the sailors in his watch did when he went forward. It was the "black sheep" of the crew—the same one who pointed out the trapper's supposed hiding-place in the bow-boat. His name was Gardener, but some one had christened him Calamity, and that was what he was generally called. Some of the crew had warned Lucas· and Barton to be very careful what they said in this man's presence. He was the captain's pet. He was never punished like the rest, and the reason probably was because he made it his business to keep the officers posted in everything that was said and done in the forecastle.

"Well, Gentleman Black," said Calamity, as Frank approached the windlass around which the watch were gathered, "how do you like the taste you have had of the Tycoon's discipline? You can't come soldiering aboard here with your airs and your graces——"

"Belay that!" cried the coxswain, jumping to his feet. "You're a soldier yourself and a tale-bearer besides, Calamity, and any more such language as that will breed a row that'll have to be settled by you and me the very first time we get ashore. That's a word with a bark on it!"

Calamity, like the coward he was, slunk back out of sight immediately, and in a few minutes got up and walked away.

CHAPTER IX.

"THERE SHE BLOWS."

IT soon became evident to all on board the Tycoon that Captain Barclay—that was the name of the master of the ship—was in a great hurry. Whaling captains, while on fishing-grounds, generally try to get over as much space as they can while daylight lasts, and to remain as nearly in one spot as possible during the night. By following this plan they can hunt over every mile of the ground, and lose no chance of finding the game of which they are in search. Captain Barclay, however, carried all the sail he could crowd, both night and day. The old sailors, Lucas and Barton among the rest, knew where he was going, and when Frank heard them express their opinions he had new cause for uneasiness.

"He's bound for the Sandwich Islands," said Lucas, one day. "He hasn't got men enough aboard here to do anything, and he's going after a crew."

"Then we can make up our minds that we have seen the last of the Stranger," said Frank.

"Why, bless you," said Lucas, "I never did expect to see her again. I never said so before because I saw that you kept hankering after her, and I wanted you to keep your spirits up as long as you could."

Frank's last hope was gone now, and it was only by a great effort of will that he kept himself from giving away utterly to his despondent feelings. "I have seen the last of my friends," thought he. "I have no one to rely on except myself. I must drag out a miserable existence here till I see a chance to escape, and then get home as best I can. I might just as well make up my mind to it."

And he did. He accepted what he believed to be the inevitable, as gracefully as he could, and worked hard to keep his thoughts from wandering back to the pleasant little cabin of the Stranger, in which he had spent so many happy hours. He learned rapidly when once he made up his mind to it, and won many a word of praise and encouragement from Lucas and Barton, who declared that he was as handy as a pocket in a shirt. His services speedily attracted the attention of the mate, who one day addressed him something after this fashion, only using much stronger language—

"I have half a mind to trice you up, Gentleman Black !"

It happened just after a sudden squall, which struck the ship and threw her over almost to her beam ends. The topsails were clewed up, and when the crew were ordered aloft, Frank was the first to mount the rigging. He made his way to the main royal, and stowed it as quickly and neatly as if he had been accustomed to the business all his life. He had learned this part of a seaman's duty more readily than the rest, because he took the most interest in it. He felt excited and exhilarated when he found himself clinging to the swaying yard, with the wind whistling about his ears and the white-caps rolling beneath him, while the ship lay over at such

11

an angle that, had he lost his hold, he would have fallen into the water thirty feet from her side. He was always among the first to respond to an order to reef or furl topsails, and perhaps he liked this duty best because there was danger in it.

Having performed the work of stowing the royal, Frank descended to the deck, where he was met by the first officer, who had kept his eye on him while he was aloft. "Yes, sir, I've the best notion in the world to trice you up!" he repeated.

"What for, sir?" asked Frank, opening his eyes in great surprise.

The young sailor was well satisfied with the work he had just performed, and wondered what he had done that was wrong. By strict attention to his work he had thus far succeeded in keeping out of any serious difficulty since the affair of the hand-spike. True, he had been sworn at, had been sent aloft several times to slush down the masts, and had worked industriously for three hours knocking the rust off the anchor, and all because the mate thought he was a trifle too "airy" sometimes; but these were light punishments compared with those which some of the men received. He had seen a sailor knocked down with a belaying pin as fast as he could get up, and another hauled up by the wrists until he swung clear of the deck, and a fifty-pound snatch-block made fast to his feet.

"I am not conscious of having done anything out of the way," continued Frank.

"O, your conscience don't trouble you, then," angrily exclaimed the officer, who did not understand Frank's fine language. "Well, your back will trouble you in less than a minute if you use any jaw to me."

"I meant, sir, that I didn't know I had done anything wrong," exclaimed Frank.

"Then why didn't you say so?" growled the mate. "You're a nice lad, I do think, to come aboard here with your smooth, oily tongue, and talk us all into believing that you are a landsman! You told me that you didn't know anything about a ship."

"Yes, sir, and I told you the truth. I have had time to learn something since then."

"So have I," said the mate. "Now listen to me, my hearty," he added, shaking his finger at Frank. "You can't soldier any longer. You'll stand your trick at the wheel and do an able seaman's duty from this hour, or I'll haze you till you'll be glad to jump overboard. Go forward, where you belong."

"Ay, ay, sir! Now I have got myself into a scrape, sure enough," thought Frank. "The very first time I receive an order I don't understand, I shall catch it. I wish I had let that royal alone."

Frank went forward and shortly afterward the first mate followed him, holding in his hand two short pieces of rope. "Gentleman Black," said he, "I need something to larrup these fellows with, when they don't act like men, and I want you to put a long splice in these ropes and a Turk's head at each end."

"Ay, ay, sir!" answered Frank. "You can't catch me in this way, my man," he added, as the mate went aft again. "If it should ever become necessary to send down the topmasts, you will find

out just how much I know about a sailor's work. I
expect I shall be the first one to be ' larruped' with
this when it is done."

Frank knew that such a rope as that he was at
work upon, could not be used anywhere about the
ship, unless it was for the purpose of beating the
men. The mate gave him the task merely to try
him; and he stationed himself, too, where he could
watch Frank in order to make sure that he did the
work himself. If he had been unable to do it, the
officer would have accused him of soldiering, and
that would have furnished him with an excuse for
punishing Frank in some way. But he missed his
object that time. The work was neatly and quickly
performed, and Frank carried it to the mate, who,
after closely examining it, grasped it with both hands
and raised it in the air. " Let me see how it will
answer the purpose for which it is intended," said
he.

If Frank had flinched or dodged, it is probable
that he would have felt the weight of the rope over
his shoulders; and it is probable, too, that the mate

would have been flat on his back the very next instant. The deck of the Tycoon was never so near being the scene of a mutiny as it was that day; and just so surely as the rope fell, just so surely would there have been trouble, and serious trouble, too— Frank did not know how serious until afterward. He little dreamed that he had eight good men to back him up. He thought he would have to depend entirely on himself, but he stood his ground as if he had had the whole crew of his old vessel, the Boxer, at his command.

The mate eyed him savagely for a moment, and then lowering the rope and telling Frank that he thought he was a very nice lad to come soldiering aboard there, when he was as able to do seaman's duty as anybody, called him some hard name and ordered him to go forward. The young sailor obeyed, glad indeed to be let off so easily; but his heart beat rapidly for a long time after that, and now and then he cast toward the officer a glance that was full of meaning.

That night all sail was made again, and while

Frank was at work on the topsail yard, Lucas, who was busy at his side, poked him with his elbow and whispered hurriedly—

"Why didn't you knock him down, cap'n?"

"Be careful," whispered Frank, in reply.

"No harm done, sir," answered the boatswain's mate. "There's nobody near us except good men and true, and I'd as soon they would hear me as not. Why didn't you knock that mate down when he raised the rope on you?"

"I had no reason for doing it," replied Frank; "but I believe I should have tried it if he had struck me. I don't think I could take a blow without resenting it. I came pretty near going in the brig that time."

"No, you didn't, not by a long sight, sir, begging your pardon for speaking so plainly," said the old sailor, with a knowing shake of his head. "If you'd a done it, you'd a been walking up and down the quarter-deck now with your thumbs in the armholes of your vest. You'd a been master of the Tycoon, sir!"

Frank looked at Lucas in amazement.

"Fact, sir," said the old boatswain's mate, earnestly. "Me and Barton got you into this scrape, all unbeknown to us who did it, and we're bound to bring you out with flying colors, I tell you!"

"Look here, Lucas," said Frank. "Now don't you or anybody else attempt——"

"Belay what I have told you and listen to more," interrupted the sailor, hastily; "and don't be breaking in on me in that way, if you please, sir, because we hain't got much time to talk. You'll never be struck, sir, I don't think, but if you are, you'll see a tidy row. The officers know who you are—me and Barton told it to the other fellows in Calamity's hearing, and he carried it back to the cabin, as we knew he would—and the cap'n would give all his old boots and throw in a pair of new ones into the bargain, if he was well rid of you. He don't want you here; you know too much."

"Well, he can easily be rid of me and you and Barton, too," said Frank. "Let him put us ashore at the Sandwich Islands. We are willing to go."

"He'll never do that, sir. You wouldn't go ashore with a stopper on your jaw, would you?"

"No, I would not," replied Frank, emphatically. "I'd tell the consul all I know about this ship and the way men are treated here, and have the captain and all his officers, except Mr. Gale, arrested. I could not be hired to keep my mouth shut."

"Ah, ha! I thought so. The cap'n knows it, too."

"What is he going to do with us?"

"None of us know. The men don't want you to leave if they've got to stay, because they say that things ain't half as bad as they were before you came aboard. We know what we're going to do, and I've been waiting for a good chance to tell you. We're going to take the ship out of the hands of these villains, and put you in command. Hold on a bit, sir," he added, seeing that Frank was about to speak; "I know just what I am saying, and it is too late to find fault, for everything is fixed. Me and Barton spoke to some of the men about it, and there's six good men besides us that you can depend on every time. We know that you've got the brains and the book-learning to see us safe through the consul's court, and we'll do just whatever you say, all except one thing : when we get the ship, Calamity and the first mate have got to go overboard. That we've struck hands on. Lay in from the yard now, sir. Keep a stiff upper lip, and don't take no slack from nobody. When you get a good ready, sing out ; and while me and Barton makes a dash for the cap'n's pistols—Calamity told us where he keeps 'em—the other six will take care of the officers on deck. We've got everything fixed, as I told you, and we're just aching to begin the work."

The old boatswain's mate followed his remarks with sundry winks, nods and contortions of his face which Frank could not understand, but which no doubt meant a good deal.

Frank descended to the deck and went through the rest of his duties like one in a dream. He had told his friends on board the Stranger that, had he been in the deserter's place, he would not have been restrained, by any fear of falling into the clutches of the law, from joining with his companions and taking the vessel out of the control of her officers. Now he was placed in a similar situation, and had only to "sing out" to make himself monarch of all he surveyed. Eight sturdy, determined men stood ready to obey his orders—a sufficient number to overpower the captain and his two tyrannical mates before they could think twice. Lucas did not have time to tell him who his friends were, but Frank believed that he could pick them all out. He had wondered at the respect which the foremast hands had shown him ever since his advent among them, and rightly attributed it to the influence of Lucas and Barton. Frank wondered if the third mate, Mr. Gale, was one of them. That officer always treated him with the utmost consideration, and once, while he was serving Frank with some clothing from the slop-chest, he so far forgot himself as to address him as "sir." He noticed the mistake as soon as he made it, but he did not recall the word. The

old boatswain's mate and coxswain were indeed resolved to bring him out of his troubles with flying
colors. They meant to promote him rapidly. Did
anybody ever hear of a person creeping in at the
hawsehole, and working his way into the captain's
berth in three weeks? Frank laughed at the idea.

"I'm a nice specimen to be put in command of
a ship," he thought. "I hardly know the topsail
halliards from the jib downhaul. But I feel better
than I did an hour ago. If my presence here really
acts as a restraint upon the captain, I am glad of it.
As long as that state of affairs continues he and his
officers are secure in their positions; but now that
I have the power to prevent it, no one shall be
triced up by the wrists with a fifty-pound weight at
his feet, or beaten as unmercifully as that man was
beaten the other day."

Frank carried a light heart from that day forward, and often wondered, when he saw the captain
in one of his angry, swearing moods, what that gentleman would think if he knew that he was treading
on a mine that was liable to be exploded at any mo-

ment. He did not have a chance to talk to Lucas again, but the sailor looked whole volumes at him every time they met, and Frank thought the old fellow meant to reproach him because he did not "sing out."

Frank by this time began to feel and look like a sailor. He had discarded his black suit and drawn a full seaman's rig from the slop-chest—red shirts, coarse trowsers, woollen stockings, heavy boots and tarpaulin. His hands were becoming hardened, so that he could haul on the ropes or take a three hours' pull about the ship, without setting his palms on fire as he had done at first. There was one thing he could not bring himself to do, and that was to go barefooted, like the rest of the crew. There was something too slovenly about that to suit Frank, who, during his experience on ship-board, had always been accustomed to see men neatly and completely dressed.

Although Captain Barclay was in a great hurry, he did not neglect to keep himself and crew in readiness to seize upon the first opportunity that was presented for adding to his stock of oil in the hold. The boats were always ready for lowering, the mast-head had been manned for two weeks; and Frank took his turn with the rest. He did his duty faithfully while acting as lookout, hoping to be the first to discover a whale. He wanted to see one; but when it came to getting into a small boat and pulling out to attack him—well, Frank wasn't so anxious for that. He drew a long breath and his heart would beat a little faster than usual whenever he thought of it. He had heard many thrilling stories related during the night-watches, and had come to the conclusion that a sperm whale was made to be looked at from a distance and not to be approached in a small boat.

One bright day Frank was sitting on the fore-royal yard, his back braced against the shroud-stay, one hand grasping the halliards and his feet swinging in the air a hundred feet above the deck. There was not a sail in sight—nothing but the ocean beneath and the blue sky above. The old boatswain's mate, who now held the position of boat-steerer, was sitting on the main-royal yard behind him, and both were keeping a bright lookout for whales. A prize of a pair of boots had been offered to the first man who raised a whale, and that to a sailor who, out of small wages, has to pay high prices for everything he draws from the slop-chest, is an object worth working for. Frank did not care for the boots— he hoped to be safely off the Tycoon long before the pair he then had on was worn out—but he did care for the honor of discovering the first spout, so he kept his eyes roaming everywhere. But half his watch had expired and he had seen nothing yet.

"Hem! hem!" said a voice behind and above him.

Frank looked around, and saw the old boatswain's mate winking and nodding at him as he always did both before and after making any confidential communication. More than that, he was holding his clenched hand against his breast, and pointing with his thumb out over the water. His meaning flashed upon Frank in an instant. His eyes scanned almost every inch of the watery waste that lay between him and the horizon, but he could see nothing that he thought looked as a spout ought to look.

"Sing out, sir!" whispered the old sailor, excitedly. "There's grease!"

"I don't see it," whispered Frank, in reply.

"What's the odds? I do. Sing out, sir!"

"There she blows!" shouted Frank, taking the old sea-dog at his word.

The flapping of the sails below him showed that his wild yell had reached the ears of at least one of the sailors on deck—the wheelsman—and that it had excited him so that he forgot for a moment to attend to his business. Then the captain's hoarse voice was heard. "Keep her steady there, can't you? Where away?"

"I am sure I don't know," said Frank, in a low tone, as he looked impatiently around.

"Three points off the weather bow!" shouted the boatswain's mate. "Three miles off and coming this way. Sperm whale. Flukes! flukes!" he added, as the whale went down with a farewell flourish of his tail.

"Dear me, I wish I could see it," thought Frank.

"Lay down from aloft!" commanded the captain. "See the boats all clear and stand by to lower."

When Frank descended to the deck in obedience to this order, he found the captain and all his mates in the rigging, the former sweeping the horizon with his glass. "There she blows!" he cried, gleefully. "Close aboard! Back the main topsail and lower away!"

Frank sprang to the falls of the boat to which he belonged, and by the time it was fairly settled in the water, he was in his seat with his oar in his hand. Much scrambling and confusion followed; but a few oaths from the captain restored order, and almost before he knew it Frank was flying over the waves in pursuit of his first whale—the whale he had raised, but which he had not yet seen.

12

CHAPTER X.

FRANK'S FIRST WHALE.

ALL this happened in much less time than we have taken to describe it. To Frank, whose brain was in a great whirl, it seemed that scarcely half a minute had elapsed after the raising of the whale, before he was in the boat and pulling for dear life. He afterwards recalled every exciting incident of that hour, and wondered that he did not feel any fear. Perhaps it was because he was too busy to think. He was not so busy, however, but that he could take note of and marvel at one thing, and that was the great change that had suddenly come over the captain. He looked and acted like a different man. He even smiled, and that was something Frank had never seen him do before. Holding the steering-oar with one hand and assist-

ing the stroke-oar with the other, he kept up a running fire of small-talk to encourage his men.

"Now, my good sons," said he, in a low voice and
in much such a tone as an affectionate father might
use, " all my ' lay' in that whale will go straight to
your credit just as soon as we get back to the ship,
if you will only put me alongside of him so that I
can get one chance at him with the lance. I declare, it has been so long since I used a lance that
I don't know how it seems, and I shall get all out
of practice if you don't take pity on me. We must
beat that other boat anyhow, and if you pull this
way, you are sure to do it. That's it; pick her
right up out of the water and walk along with her.
She isn't a feather's weight to such long-armed,
broad-shouldered fellows as you are. That's the
way to do it; only raise her just an inch higher, my
lads. She touched that wave; I felt it, didn't you?
There! she didn't touch that one and I know it.
Keep her there, my good lads. She's in the air
now. Talk about your balloons! Give me this
boat and crew and I'll go anywhere they can!"

For the first time since he came on board the
Tycoon, Frank felt like laughing. The captain
reminded him of Hans Breitman's velocipede, which,
even before it became frightened and started to run
away with its rider, went so fast that it

> "—— didn't touch the dirt, py shinks,
>   Not once in half a mile."

"Bless me, what muscles those two fellows in the
bow have got!" continued the captain, still working
at the stroke-oar with all his strength. "And how
they do twist them oars about, just as if they were
feathers! I've got to have stronger and heavier
oars made for them, I can see that, for they're
bound to break them they've got now. Ah! she
touched that wave. Lift her up in the air again,
where she belongs, and hold her there. You fellows
in the bow needn't think you can pull your end of
the boat so fast that we in the stern can't keep up
with you. By the way, is that sharp-eyed, good-
looking son of mine, who raised this whale, in the
boat?"

"Yes, sir. It was Nelson," replied Lucas, promptly.

Frank, who did not believe in sailing under false colors, was about to protest that it wasn't he at all —that Lucas himself was the lucky man—but knowing the captain's uncertain disposition, and fearing that there might be some after-settlement that would prove unpleasant for the old boatswain's mate if the truth were known, he kept silent and heard himself praised for an act that he did not perform.

"Ah! it is just like him," said the captain. "I knew there was lots in him the first time I saw him. You can't fool me in a man. I can look in his eye and read him like an open book. There's a boatsteerer's berth ahead for you, Nelson," continued the captain, too excited and impatient to think of the name he always applied to Frank in derision. "Those boots belong to you, and when we get back to the ship you go straight down to the slop-chest —I'll give you the key—and pick out whatever you want. Take everything you find there—boots, breeches, shirts and—no, no! Take the ship. She's yours! That's the way Daddy Barclay treats his sons when they do their duty by him. Now, my lads," he added, in a thrilling whisper, "he's right here somewhere below us. Lay on your oars now; keep your eyes peeled and don't let me hear so much as an eye-wink from any of you."

Frank's heart fairly came up into his mouth. The captain's harangue being ended (he had a suspicion that the skipper had kept it up on purpose to divert the minds of his crew, one of whom was as green as Frank himself), there was nothing to occupy his attention, and he had leisure to ponder upon the dangers he was about to encounter. Of course all the stories he had heard in the Tycoon's forecastle concerning the perils to which whalemen are constantly exposed, came into his mind, and to save his life he could think of nothing else. He felt as he had often felt on going into action. After the crew are called to quarters there is almost always a delay, sometimes longer and sometimes shorter, before the first gun is fired, and to most men

that is worse than the battle itself. They are glad
when it is over and the fight begins. The interval
of inactivity that came now gave the boat's crew a
chance to rest after their long, hard pull, but Frank
could scarcely endure it. He wanted the whale to
show himself at once. If he was going to cut the
boat in two with his jaw or smash it into kindling
wood with his tail, Frank wished he would be about
it and not keep him in suspense.

The whale was down a long time—so long that
even the captain became impatient. He and the
boat's crew, Frank among the rest, arose to their
feet one after the other to obtain a wider view, and
holding their oars in their hands, kept a bright
lookout in every direction. The first mate's boat
was lying about half a mile to windward, and her
crew were also standing up. The Tycoon had come
to directly in the path the whale was pursuing, and
the third officer was at the mast-head, ready to
signal to the boat's crews if the whale arose beyond
the range of their vision. Frank's eyes were everywhere, and at last something induced him to turn

them into the water close alongside the boat. He
saw something there—an immense dark-blue object,
which contrasted plainly with the paler blue of the
water. He looked again, and then glanced into the
water on the opposite side of the boat to make sure
that his eyes had not deceived him. The sea on
that side was all the same color, and that proved
that there was something under the boat. He
nudged Lucas with his elbow and pointed to it.
The old sailor looked, and instantly every particle
of color fled from his face. But he had nerve, if he
was frightened, plenty of it, too, and it showed
itself in the firm grasp he laid upon his harpoon.
The time for action had arrived.

"He's coming," thought Frank, while the oar he
held in his grasp seemed to turn into lead, so heavy
did it feel to his weakened arm. "I always supposed a whale was black."

The boat header's action attracted the attention
of the captain, who, following the direction of his
gaze gave a sudden start and waved his hand to the
crew. The men quickly seated themselves and

dropped their oars softly in the row-locks. The temptation to look over his shoulder was almost irresistible, but fearing that if he did, his courage, which was rapidly oozing out at the ends of his fingers, would give away altogether, Frank resolutely controlled himself and kept his eyes fixed on the captain's face.

"There he is," cried the skipper, a moment afterward. "Throw it at him and go overboard if you miss him."

The old sailor obeyed the order to the very letter. He threw his harpoon, missed his object and went overboard. Whether it was for the reason that the boat was unsteady, or because the seaman was too badly frightened to stand firmly on his feet, or because his hand had lost its skill during the years that had passed since he struck his last whale, it is hard to tell. Perhaps all these things combined operated to bring about the events that followed. At any rate the iron went wild and the old boatswain's mate turned a complete back somersault and disappeared over the side. He rose immediately, however, and

Frank catching sight of him as a wave carried him past the boat, promptly thrust his oar out to him.

The captain was almost beside himself with fury. He did not act or talk quite so much like an affectionate father as he did a short time before. He tore off his hat, trampled it under his feet and shook all over with rage. "He missed him as sure as I'm a sinner," he sputtered, hardly able to speak plainly. "If I had him aboard the ship I would trice him up for a week. Let the fool go," he roared with a long string of heavy adjectives, as Frank tried to place the blade of his oar in the old sailor's grasp. "A man that'll get up on his legs and tumble overboard while the boat is standing still, is of no use aboard a vessel of mine; so let him go down among the sharks, where he belongs. We're well rid of—Stern all! Stern for your lives! Well done, my son. You've been in this business before, and you are my boat-header from this day out."

The change in the captain's tone was brought about by an action on Frank's part that was unexpected, even to himself. He scarcely knew he did it until after it was done. Lucas, having missed his first throw and gone overboard, had no chance for a second attempt, and unless somebody took his place on the instant, the game was likely, if he did not escape altogether, to lead them a long, hard race before they could come up with him again. It required an emergency to show what Frank was made of. He never waited to take a second thought, but throwing his oar to the boatswain's mate—he knew it would keep him afloat until the boat could pick him up—he jumped to his feet, catching up the extra harpoon as he arose.

When his face was turned toward the bow of the boat, Frank saw a sight that was well calculated to shake stronger nerves than his—a sperm whale coming up on a breach almost within an oar's length of him. His huge bulk was shooting up into the air, and he did not even make a ripple in the water as he arose. But when he fell on his side, as he did a moment later, he created something more than a ripple. He raised waves that

threatened to swamp the boat, and made a noise
that would have given Frank some idea of the immense weight of the monster, if he had not been
too highly excited and alarmed to have any ideas at
all.

As the whale fell into the water—fortunately he
fell away from the boat—Frank's harpoon was
launched into the air, and being thrown with all the
force his sinewy arms could give it, and flying true
to its aim, was buried to the socket in the side of
the whale.   The next instant the young harpooner
was thrown flat among the thwarts by the sudden
start backward which the crew gave the boat in
obedience to the captain's order " Stern all !"   He
heard something whistling through the air, and
looked up just in time to see the whale's flukes dis-
appearing in a pile of foam.   How he opened his
eyes at the sight of them !   They would have measured more feet across than the boat measured in
length.   The whale gave the water an angry slap,
raising a sea that would have filled the boat had not
the bow been promptly brought around toward it,

and then started down into the depths at the rate of a mile in six minutes, the line fairly smoking as it whizzed through the lead-lined groove. Frank held his breath while he gazed at it. It looked like a streak of blue flame, so swiftly did it run out. If it caught on anything, the boat and all her crew would be a hundred feet under water in an instant's time.

The young harpooner did not hear any of the words of praise and promises of reward which the delighted skipper shouted at him. He did not hear anything but the hissing of the line as it ran through the groove in the bow. He lay on the bottom perfectly stupefied, until he was aroused by the touch of somebody's hand.

When the captain gave the order to " Stern all," the crew sent the boat within reach of Lucas, who laid hold of the gunwale, and worked his way along to the bow, where he belonged. Attracting Frank's attention by a pull at his trowsers, he was hauled into the boat, and took his seat, looking not a little crestfallen. He caught up a hatchet lying near, and held it in his hand in readiness to cut the line in case it fouled while running out. Frank also seated himself, and then began to think about what he had done. No one in the boat could have been more surprised at it.

"I don't want any more of this," said he, mentally. "It is just awful. I can't stand it. While that fellow was shooting up toward the clouds he looked like a church-steeple turned wrong end up. He must be a hundred and fifty feet long—perhaps more. Who would have thought that I had courage enough to send that harpoon at him?"

Here Frank looked over his shoulder as if to satisfy himself that he had really performed the feat. There could be no mistake about it. The line was still running out, and Lucas was watching it while hauling in the harpoon with which he had missed the whale.

"I believe I did do it," thought Frank. "He is black after all. It was the water that made him look so blue. I wouldn't do it again to be made owner of the finest fleet of ships that ever floated!"

"Nelson," said the captain, and now that Frank's mind was settled a little he was able to pay attention to him, "whatever I've got that you want, just ask for it and it is yours. Don't be bashful or stand on ceremony with your Daddy Barclay. Take a big bite if you want to."

"I have only one favor to ask, captain," replied Frank, suddenly tempted to strike while the iron was hot, although he knew it would be quite useless, "and that is——"

"Well, slack away lively, and let it come out on the run," said the captain, as Frank hesitated a moment, wondering how he could word the request so that the skipper would not get angry at him. "Speak it out."

"I should be greatly obliged if you would set me and the two men who were shanghaied with me, ashore at the first port we make," said Frank. "We shall use the right the law gives us, and ask to see the consul as soon as we get there."

Frank's only motive in saying this was to let the captain know that he understood the law applying

to the rights of seamen; and he said it at that time
because he did not know that he would ever have
another chance, this being the first opportunity he
had ever had to exchange a word with the master
of the Tycoon.   If there is anything an officer thoroughly detests it is a "sea lawyer" among his crew.
One of these gentry will keep a ship's company in
hot water from the time the voyage begins until it
is ended; and his presence acts as a restraint upon
the captain and his mates, who, if they are disposed
to be tyrannical, expect to escape the consequences
through the sailor's ignorance of their rights.
Frank knew this, and he was in hopes that if he let
the captain see that he knew what his privileges
were, and that he intended to insist on having them,
the skipper would be glad to get rid of him with as
little delay as possible.

The master of the Tycoon had not a word to say
in reply to this request, but the look he gave Frank
satisfied the latter that if he had not spoken at the
right time to further his own interests, he had
spoken at the right time to make the captain angry.

He did not offer Frank any more rewards after that.

The line continued to run out with great rapidity for a few minutes, then the speed gradually decreased until it remained motionless, and the actions of the captain and his crew indicated that the whale was soon expected to make his appearance at the surface again. He came very speedily, and much too close to the boat for the comfort and safety of its crew. Seen through Frank's frightened eyes, his head looked like a small mountain rising out of the water. His mouth was wide open, showing a milk-white cavity large enough to take in the boat and all its crew, and Frank gathered from something Lucas said that he was ugly and had made up his mind to do some mischief. The sequel proved that the old sailor was right. The monster began operations at once by striking out with his long, sword-like jaw, which to Frank's great amazement he worked sideways, instead of up and down, and followed it up with a tremendous sweep of his tail that, had he succeeded in planting the blow where he

13

wanted it, would have made an end of his enemies in a hurry. But both these dangers were escaped. His jaw just touched the bow of the boat, and the blow from his flukes was avoided by the vigilance of the captain and the prompt obedience of the crew, who quickly backed the boat out of his reach. Apparently satisfied with the demonstrations he had made, the whale got under way and made off at an astonishing rate of speed, the harpoon which Frank had planted still fast in his side.

The bow-oarsman now had a duty to perform, and he set about it without waiting for orders. It was to overhaul the line and draw the boat up alongside the whale, so that the captain, who stood ready to change places with the harpooner, could use his lance. He rapidly drew in the line, taking care to lay it down clear of everything, so that it would not kink or get foul in case the whale sounded again, and soon had the slack all in. Then he felt a strain upon it, and an instant afterward the line was whipped out of the water with such force that it was drawn as tight as a bow-string, and the spray flew from it in a perfect shower.

"Hold fast to it, my son," yelled the captain. "Keep every inch you get, and get every inch you can. We'll have a sleigh-ride now, and such a one as landsmen know nothing about."

For a moment the strain was fearful, and Frank's power of muscle was tested to the utmost. It seemed to him that if the harpoon did not draw or the line break, his arms would be pulled off. Letting go was something he did not think of; but he knew he could not retain his hold much longer, so in spite of the old mate's warning gestures, he passed a bight of the line around a thwart and held it there. By this time the boat began to move, and the strain was somewhat lessened.

Now began a novel ride, which Frank thought he could have enjoyed if he had only had leisure to give his attention to it. A whale can move at tremendous speed for a short distance, and this one went at such a rate that the boat buried her bow in the waves, and rolled back great masses of foam, which, spreading out over the surface of the water, gave it the appearance of a bank of snow. Perhaps it was this that first caused the sailors to call a ride of this kind a sleigh-ride. But Frank had no time to see what was going on around him. He had work to perform; and it *was* work to haul a heavy boat containing six men through the waves against such resistance as the whale created by the high rate of speed he kept up. The line was wet and slippery, and Frank's hands, which he had fondly hoped were pretty well hardened by this time, soon began to feel the effects of it.

In the first lesson he received while manœuvring about the "dummy whale," Frank had been instructed how to adjust the line to make the boat move side by side with a running whale and at a short distance from it, and he struggled hard to bring the boat in that position; but the line came in very slowly, and sometimes when he was almost on the point of accomplishing his object, an unusually large wave striking the bow or a sudden spurt on the part of the frantic beast in front, would tear the line from his hands in spite of all he could do to prevent it.

At length, after Frank had worked his best for nearly an hour without once pausing for breath, and the line had been drawn through his hands for the third time, the captain's small stock of patience was all exhausted, and he began to relieve his mind by uttering heavy oaths. "Coward!" he yelled, stamping his feet as if he were trying to knock a hole through the bottom of the boat. "If you are afraid to put me alongside that whale, jump overboard and give place to a better man. You're fixing your back for a rope's end as soon as you get aboard the ship!"

Frank and the old boatswain's mate exchanged quick glances, one elevating his eye-brows, and the other drawing his down. The first meant: "If he tries it will you sing out?" and Frank by his answering scowl meant: "I will." Not a word was passed, but each understood the other perfectly.

CHAPTER XI.

CUTTING IN AND TRYING OUT.

THE high-spirited Frank, smarting under a sense of injustice, and hardly able to bear the pain occasioned by his lacerated hands, suddenly became very reckless. The captain had no excuse for talking to him in that style after what he had done. A coward would not have been likely to take a defeated harpooner's place and plunge an iron into the first whale he had ever seen, and neither would he have worked as hard as Frank did to bring the boat into position; and that he *did* work, the crimson stains his hands left on the rope abundantly proved.

"I have had this boat alongside that whale three times," said Frank, to himself, "and if I get her there again she'll stay, unless something breaks. I'll make all fast; and if the whale goes down and takes us to the bottom with him, it can't be helped. I'll see who will be the first to act like a coward, the captain or I."

Had Frank carried this reckless resolve into execution, and had the whale sounded as soon as the line was made fast, the boat would not have been emptied of her crew more quickly than she was a moment later. The whale threw his flukes about in the most spiteful manner, but finding that he could not reach the boat with them, he gave signs of a change of tactics which created a panic among all the crew except Frank and the old boatswain's mate. Frank was not frightened because he did not understand them—in his case ignorance was bliss—but the sailor did, and he did not turn white this time either. He was about to be given an opportunity to make amends for his previous defeat, and he was ready to improve it.

"He's going to 'mill,'" said he in a low tone as he picked up his harpoon. "Don't slack an inch till I get a dart at him."

Before Frank could ask an explanation the whale

raised his huge head from the water, dropped his
jaw at right angles with his body and turning as
quickly as a flash, started off across the course he
had been pursuing. Frank, who was sitting with
face forward so that he had a fair view of the whale
and could see every move he made, stared at him in
amazement; and while awaiting the issue of events
with a calmness that surprised himself, eagerly responded to the harpooner's entreaty to haul in
faster, although he believed that certain death
awaited him. It seemed as if the boat would run
squarely into the whale's mouth.

"Slack that line!" roared the captain, suddenly
stopping his swearing and speaking in an imploring
tone of voice. "Slack that line, and may He 'en
have mercy on us! Stern all, for life!"

Frank dropped the line, which seemed like a coal
of fire in his hands, and the men laid out their
strength on the oars till they fairly snapped. The
first stroke stopped the boat's headway and the
second started her on the back track, but not in
time to escape the danger that threatened her.

THE AIR SEEMED TO BE LITERALLY FILLED WITH PIECES OF PLANKS, HARPOONS, ROPES, AND LANCES.

Before Lucas could throw his harpoon the whale's jaw swept around like a scythe, and striking the boat in the side overturned her in an instant, smashing in the planks as if they had been pasteboard, and tumbling those of the crew who did not jump out into the water.

From the crest of a wave on which he struck, Frank turned to look at the whale and see what had become of his companions. The monster was bringing his tail into play now. With one fierce upward sweep of his huge flukes he lifted the battered boat out of the water, and the captain, who had clung to the wreck, was going up with it. The air seemed to be literally filled with pieces of planks, harpoons, ropes and lances. The crew had all escaped without injury—at least they were all able to swim, for Frank counted four frightened faces bobbing about on the waves near him. He had some idea now of the strength and ferocity a whale could display when he once set about it. He made up his mind, too, that men must be simply foolhardy to willingly follow any such business as whaling. Otherwise how could they bring themselves to engage with such a monster as this, against whose tremendous power, which he had just seen exerted with such telling effect, their strength was as nothing?

To say that Frank was frightened would not begin to tell how he felt. How helpless he was! How completely the waves baffled his mad efforts to get out of the reach of his dangerous foe, and how like straws they seemed in the path of the whale which skimmed through them as easily as a bird passes through the air! Then how frightened everybody else was, if he might judge by the pale faces he saw about him, and the frantic attempts the men made to swim away. If those who were accustomed to such scenes and such dangers were so nearly overcome with terror, it was time for a novice to show signs of fear.

"Look out, Nelson!" cried Lucas, suddenly. "Look out! He's——"

The old boatswain's mate no doubt meant to say something else, but he did not stay on top of the water long enough to say it. He ducked his head and went down like lead, making desperate struggles to go faster. Frank cast one frightened glance over his shoulder and went down too. The whale had turned again and was coming directly toward him, rolling from side to side and slashing from right to left with his jaw, describing at each stroke a circle thirty-two feet in diameter. There was no time to swim out of his reach. His only chance for life was to go below him. How Frank blessed his lucky stars at that moment that deep diving and swimming long distances under water were two of his accomplishments! He went as far down as he could, stayed under as long as he could hold his breath, and came up almost strangled. He was out of danger. The battered boat was twenty feet away and the whale a hundred feet still farther off, and moving rapidly toward the ship. The men were all clinging to the boat to keep themselves afloat, and Frank swam up and joined them.

All this while the men in the mate's boat had been doing their best with sail and oars to get near

enough to the whale to take part in the fight, but
without success.   Now, however, they had an opportunity offered them, for the whale had doubled
on his course, and if he did not take it into his head
to turn again, he would pass their boat at such a
distance that they would have a chance at him with
their harpoons.   The mate prepared for it by ordering one man to take down the sail while, the rest
still tugged at the oars.   He did not even look
toward the disabled boat or ask if the crew wanted
assistance.

"These whalemen are a heartless lot," thought
Frank.   "If I were in command of that boat I
think I should save my shipmates first; but I suppose that officer thinks we are not worth as much
as the whale.   Men can be had any day for the
asking, and if a few of them lose their lives
what's the odds?   Nobody misses them.   But
whales are not as plenty as they used to be, and if
one of them is lost it is something to be sorry
for."

Frank's meditations were interrupted and his

attention called from the chase by the actions of one the men near him, who suddenly began to make desperate efforts to climb into the boat. He persisted in spite of the angry orders and oaths of the skipper, who stormed and threatened to no purpose. The man was almost beside himself with fear.

" What has come over him all at once ?" asked Frank, of the man at his side. " He was quiet enough a moment ago."

" He had a narrow escape from a shark once," replied the sailor, " and I guess he has just thought of it."

" Well, I wish from the bottom of my heart that he hadn't thought of it at all," said Frank, " or else that I had not asked you any questions, for I have new cause for alarm now. I wonder if a sailor can turn in any direction without finding himself confronted by some deadly peril ?"

" He might if he's a merchantman, but not if he is a whaler," was the comforting reply.

" If I had thought of sharks I never could have dived under that whale," continued Frank.

"O, 'tain't time for 'em to be on hand yet; but you'll see 'em coming like a flock of sheep just as soon as that fellow begins to spout blood."

"Ay, that you will," said another. "I was hanging on to a stove boat once, just as we are now, and the sharks, I never see the beat of 'em in all my born days, come up——"

"Well, if they got hold of anybody, I don't want to know it," interrupted Frank, with a shudder. "Can't you talk about something else?"

"Take that!" shouted the captain, who was narrowly watching the chase. "And that!" he added, a moment afterward. "He's fast again, and we are sixty barrels of grease ahead."

Frank looked up to see what had called forth these exclamations from the captain, and was just in time to catch a glimpse of the mate's harpooner as he threw his second iron into the whale. He had three harpoons in him now, and Frank gathered from the remarks the men made that his capture was considered certain. He lashed the water furiously with his tail, raising an immense pile of spray and foam, and when it disappeared he was out of sight.

"Now look out for breakers," said Lucas, "for there's no knowing where he will come up, and he's ugly if he is little. We know that, don't we?"

"Little!" repeated Frank, who remembered that he had compared the beast to a church-steeple, and estimated his length at one hundred and fifty feet; "how big is he?"

"The cap'n says sixty barrels."

"I mean, how long is he?"

"O, I don't know. I never took the measure of one. I ain't a tailor."

"Did you ever know of one larger than this?"

"Many a one. I heard of one once that ran a hundred and thirty-five barrels, but I didn't see him. The biggest one I ever struck or saw struck turned out a hundred and fifteen barrels."

"Almost twice as large as this one," thought Frank, hardly able to believe his ears. "Whew! I will never sail another foot in the Tycoon after we reach the Sandwich Islands. If a youngster can kick up a row like this, what could a full grown one do ? What *wouldn't* he do if he got mad ?"

Frank was greatly relieved to hear one of the men say at that moment that the ship was coming down to pick them up. It was anything but pleasant to be placed in such a situation as that in which he and his companions were placed just then, immersed to their necks in salt water, every wave making a clean breach over them, nothing but a battered boat to keep them afloat, an enraged and ugly whale in close proximity, and a school of hungry sharks expected to arrive every moment. On the contrary, it was a situation well calculated to inspire terror.

The good ship never seemed to move so slowly before, but she came up with them at last, a boat pulled by two men came out to their relief, and in ten minutes more the wrecked boat was on deck in possession of the carpenter, and the exhausted men were in the forecastle, exchanging their wet clothes for dry ones. When Frank went on deck again the whale was in his " flurry," which, upon

inquiry, he found to be a sailor's way of saying
"death struggle." The mate and his crew had
made short work of him, and Frank came up too
late to see the lance used. The whale was swimming in a circle at a surprising rate of speed,
pounding the sea with his flukes, spouting blood
from his blow-hole, and rolling from side to side as
if trying to reach his enemies with his jaw. His
fury increased for a few seconds, then gradually
lessened, and finally the captured monster rolled
over and lay motionless on the water. "Fin out!"
cried all the sailors on the Tycoon, which was
equivalent to saying, "he is dead." Then all joined
in a yell of triumph, except Frank. He could not
help feeling sorry for the conquered leviathan, who
had battled so strongly for his life, and told himself that it was a mean business altogether.

"Men who can torture a beast like that to death
and feel no remorse over it, would serve their fellow creatures the same way if they had a good
chance," was what he said to himself. "I know
now how it comes that the captain and his two
14

mates are so brutal. They have practiced on whales so long that they have no feeling left."

Now came the work of making fast to the whale, which was begun as soon as the ship was brought alongside of it. Frank did not see how it was done, for he was kept busy at something else. When he had leisure to look over the side he found the game secured by a chain, one end of which was fastened just above the tail, and the other led through a hawsehole to the bitts. He could see the whole length of him now, and had it not been for the three harpoons sticking in his back and side, he could hardly have brought himself to believe that it was the same whale that smashed his boat. He looked very much smaller, and the reason was because he had something to compare him with.

And now came the most disagreeable part of a whaleman's duties—the cutting in and trying out. The first consists in removing the blubber from the body of the whale, cutting off the head and bailing out the spermaceti; and the next in rendering out the oil in the try-kettles. Lucas said that, as the day was far spent, the work ought not to be commenced until the next morning. The crew could then have a good night's sleep after their hard work in the boats, and be fresh and ready for the laborious duties before them; but Captain Barclay thought differently. He never cared for the comfort of his men, so he ordered them to begin at once.

How long it took to do the work Frank never knew, for he was too busy and too completely tired out to keep track of the days. The crew was so small that every man was required to handle the blubber as it was hauled aboard by the tackles; and when that was all stowed, and the carcass cut adrift, the watches were lengthened into six (they were often nearer eight) hours each, and the trying out began. Frank did not wonder that the men grew quarrelsome, and that more than one of them had to be driven to his work with a rope's end, being compelled, as they were, to work almost twenty hours out of the twenty-four. He thought often of what he had read concerning the fiendish ingenuity

displayed by the Chinese in inventing modes of torture for those who disobey their laws, and told himself that some of them must have served their
time in a whale-ship, and there learned by experience the misery to which a person is subjected when
deprived of sleep. Frank would not have resented
a blow himself now, he was too weak and dispirited;
but he would have given all he ever hoped to
possess, if he could have lain down in all the oil
and dirt of the blubber-room, and had a good sound
nap. The work was made harder by the captain's
great desire to fill up the hold as soon as possible.
He kept the mast-head manned all day by some of
the crew who ought to have been allowed to go
below to rest, and swore at them roundly because
they did not raise another whale; although it is
hard to tell what good it would have done if they
had discovered a school of them, for in their exhausted condition they never could have endured a
lengthened struggle with one. Frank often thought,
after it was all over, that the only thing that sus-
tained him during that week, was the sweet, sound

sleep he had every time he acted as lookout. Seated on the royal yard, a hundred and more feet in the air, with his back against the stay and a rope passed about his waist to keep him from falling off, he would slumber like a log, leaving the whales, if there were any, to spout in peace. The rest of the crew being equally sleepy and careless, no more whales were raised, and Frank was glad of it.

"I can't stand this, Mr. Gale," said Frank one day, when the third officer came into the blubber-room where he was at work, "and I won't."

"You won't?"

"No, sir. I have never done any soldiering since I have been aboard here, but I shall do it hereafter."

"Do you know that you are talking to the third mate of this ship?" demanded Mr. Gale, who seemed surprised at Frank's strong language.

"I do, sir, and I am not afraid to speak to you more plainly still."

"Why ain't you."

"Because I know that you will neither get angry at what I say nor repeat it."

"Well, I suppose I ought to give you a good blowing-up for your impudence," said the mate, who had to smile in spite of himself, "but I can't."

"No, of course you can't. You know I have cause to be down on every officer of this ship except you, and that I will some day be in a position to make them smart for it. You know what they have done."

"Well, we'll drop that. It ain't for me to talk about the doings of my superiors. I came down here to tell you something that'll liven you up a bit, may be. We shall sight the Islands in a few days, and the old man is going to put you ashore."

"Good for him," exclaimed Frank, who was wide awake in an instant. "How about Lucas and Barton ?"

"Don't talk so loud. The masts, bulkheads and everything else have ears in this ship. I don't know about them. He didn't say."

" They must go if I go," said Frank. " I shall need them for witnesses."

" But you mustn't call any witnesses. If you go ashore at Honolulu, you must keep still and say nothing."

" O, I must! Do you think that's the sort of fellow I am? Must I let a man kidnap me, carry me away from my friends to some out-of-the-way part of the world, and then, in order to gain the liberty of which he has deprived me and which rightfully belongs to me, promise him that he shall go scot free? Must he be allowed to run at large to try the same game upon somebody else, and perhaps abuse and maltreat him until he jumps overboard, as those two men did shortly before you reached Fr'isco? No, sir! He be jerked as high as the strong arm of the law can lift him, and that's pretty high. A thousand dollars fine and a long term in the penitentiary are the rewards that surely await him, and perhaps he can be tried for manslaughter. I am bound to have my liberty, Mr. Gale, and I shall get it without entering into any such agreement as that. If anybody makes promises, it will be Captain Barclay."

Frank, being thoroughly aroused, clattered away in spite of all the officer's attempts to interrupt him. He could not have told why he said what he did toward the last. Perhaps he had a prophetic vision, during which the thrilling scenes that were so soon to be enacted were plainly portrayed. At any rate the words came into his mind, and he uttered them regardless of consequences. He was about to say something more, but an emphatic and warning gesture from the mate stopped him.

Frank looked up and saw Calamity's sinister face peering down the hatchway. His first impulse was to knock him over with the handle of the blubber-knife for playing eavesdropper; but the vacant expression on the man's countenance induced the hope that perhaps he had only just come there, and had heard nothing he could make use of.

"Look here," exclaimed Mr. Gale suddenly, doubling up his huge fist and shaking it at Frank, "I am an officer of this ship and you must respect

me, or I'll teach you manners. Put a ' sir' in when
you speak to me. As for Cap'n Barclay promising
you them boots, I reckon you'll get 'em when this
work is done; and if I hand 'em to you you'll
get 'em over your head for your impudence !"

" O, is that you down there, Mr. Gale ?" exclaimed Calamity. " It is so dark I couldn't see you.
The captain wants you on deck."

The officer lingered a moment to add a few words
to what he had already said, and then mounted the
ladder leading to the deck, while Frank went on
separating the fleshy fibres from the blubber.

CHAPTER XII.

HOW FRANK SAW THE CONSUL.

FRANK knew why it was that Mr. Gale changed his tone and manner so suddenly. It was Calamity's presence that made him do it. The mate knew that if this man had overheard any of the conversation between himself and Frank he would go straight to the captain with it; and it would never do to let the skipper know that one of his officers had been so familiar with a foremast hand. It would not only make it unpleasant for himself, but Frank would most likely be punished for daring to express himself so plainly. Mr. Gale hoped that by speaking roughly and flourishing his fists in the most approved quarter-deck style, he could put Calamity on the wrong scent, and make him believe that he had been taking Frank to task for some-

thing.   But the eavesdropper understood all that,
and was much too smart to be deceived by any such
artifice.

"They can't shut up my eyes in no such way as
that," said he, with a knowing shake of his head.
"I heard it all, and see through their backing and
filling as plainly as they do. I've got a chance to
square yards with both of them now, and I knew
it would come if I only waited long enough and
kept my eyes and ears open. That Gentleman
Black is so stuck up that he won't notice a common
fellow like me, and Mr. Gale jawed me the other
day and called me a soldier and a lubber. Won't
there be a healthy old row here directly? I guess
yes."

There certainly would be if this man was able to
bring it about, for he took great delight in such
things, especially when he knew that he was out
of danger himself. He hunted up the captain without delay, and the latter saw at a glance that he
had something to tell him. "What is it, Gardner?"
said he. (Behind his back the captain always

called him Calamity, and in his heart despised him as cordially as any of the crew did.) "Your face is full of news."

"You said you would put Nelson ashore at the Sandwich Islands if he'd keep still and say nothing, didn't you, cap'n?" began Calamity.

"Yes, I did," replied the skipper, interested at once. "Have you been pumping him?"

"No, but Mr. Gale has, and he says he'll hang you as high as the strong arm of the law can hist you. He can't be hired to keep his mouth shut. He told Mr. Gale so, and him and Mr. Gale were talking mighty familiar and friendly like—too much so, for it don't look well for an officer to do such things."

"What did Mr. Gale say?"

"I didn't hear what he said at first, but I saw him winking and nodding, and when he saw me looking down the hatchway, he began to jaw Nelson about them boots you promised him for raising that whale. But he did it just to fool me."

"Then Nelson is going to hang me, is he?"

"Yes, and he wants Barton and Lucas for witnesses. He says he'll tell the consul everything that's been done aboard this ship, and you shan't be let loose any longer to haze men till they jump overboard."

"Go for'ard; go for'ard," said the captain, hastily.

"Aha!" thought Calamity, as he returned to his duties, "that was a home-thrust. I must say he took it easier than I thought he would. I must say this too for Gentleman Black, that since he's been on board, there haven't been so many men triced up or knocked down with handspikes, and the grub has been better than it ever was before. Now I'll tell you what's the truth," added Calamity, slapping his knee as he leaned over and looked under the try-pots, "Gentleman Black is master here, if he is nothing but a foremast hand, and that's what's the matter. That's the reason the old man takes things so easy, and don't go ripping and tearing around the way he used to. I wonder if I hadn't better make friends with him!"

Meanwhile the work of trying-out went slowly on, and contrary to Calamity's expectations, though not much to his surprise, the captain took no steps to punish Mr. Gale and Frank for the conversation they had had in the blubber-room. Indeed he thought he could see a change in the skipper and in the two mates. The former very rarely went off into one of his fits of rage now, and the mates seemed to treat the men a trifle more like human beings. Every one of the crew noticed it, and Lucas, after sundry winks and nods, told Frank in confidence that something was going to happen very shortly. And sure enough, something did happen, but it was not just what the old sailor thought it would be.

Finally the last barrel of oil was lowered into the hold, and the captain, to the surprise of his men, who had never known him to be guilty of an act of kindness before, sent all the crew except a boat-steerer's watch below to sleep. And a glorious sleep they had too after their days and nights of labor. Frank felt like another person when he

came on deck in the morning, and went to work
with a light heart to assist in cleaning up the ship.
This required perseverance and the outlay of a
good deal of strength, but it was done in good time,
and when the deck was wiped down and the bright-
work cleaned, the Tycoon looked as though she had
never been near a whale. By this time land was
in plain sight, and Frank and Lucas found opportunity to hold several whispered consultations as to
the course they ought to pursue to secure their
release. On two points Frank had made up his
mind: If he went ashore, Lucas and Barton must
be permitted to go also; and he would not purchase
his freedom by entering into any agreement whatso-
ever with the captain of the Tycoon. The last one
of these consultations was broken up by the sudden
appearance of the third mate.

"Nelson," said he, "the old man wants to see
you in the cabin."

"Ay, ay, sir!" replied Frank.

"And you had better take a friend's advice,"
continued the officer, in a low tone, as the young

sailor was about to pass him, " and agree to what he has to propose."

Frank did not say whether he would or not. He wanted first to hear what it was that the captain had to propose. He went into the cabin and found the skipper and his two mates seated at a table there. The former had some shipping articles before him, and the first mate was reading a well-thumbed copy of Bowditch. This was encouraging. If the three officers had been examining the law, they no doubt learned that they were liable to some heavy penalties for what they had done.

"Nelson," said the captain, as Frank came in, " you haven't signed articles yet."

" No, sir," said Frank.

" Well, just put your name to them now," continued the captain, pushing them across the table. " There's a chair and there's a pen."

" I beg to be excused, sir," replied Frank.

" Won't you do it ?"

" I'd rather not, sir."

" Suit yourself," said the captain indifferently.

"I am only advising you as a friend. You will lose your work if you don't. You can't collect a cent from the ship if you stay aboard of her ten years."

"I am sorry to differ with you, sir, but I know better than that."

"Be careful how you speak," said the captain, starting up in his chair. "I have stood a good deal from you, and you don't want to say too much. You are not talking to Mr. Gale now."

"You haven't stood more than I have, sir," returned Frank. "It is high time I should speak plainly, as I never had the chance before and may never have it again. I know that when seamen are shipped on American whaling vessels without the rate of their pay being specified, they are entitled on their discharge in a foreign port, to the sum of twenty dollars a month as extra wages."

"How do you happen to know so much about law, Nelson?" asked the first mate.

"The way I happen to know so much about these matters is because I read up, expecting at one time

15

to go as consul's clerk to some port in the Mediter-ranean."

The captain and his mates opened their eyes and looked at one another. Here was a foremast hand who must hold a high social position when he was ashore, else he would not number among his friends those who had influence enough to secure govern-ment appointments.

"Then you won't sign these articles?" continued the captain, after thinking a moment.

"By no means, sir. I don't want to go to sea for two or three years. I want to go ashore."

"I am willing you should go, if you will promise not to enter any complaints."

"If I should promise that, captain, I should tell a falsehood, and that is something I'll not do."

"Will a hundred dollars be any inducement to you?"

"Not the slightest."

"A hundred dollars besides your wages, I mean."

"No, sir," repeated Frank. "You are liable for

two hundred dollars for every foremast hand aboard this vessel, except Calamity."

"How do you make that out?"

"You carried them to sea without making a contract with them."

"That'll do. You can go on deck," said the captain.

"But before I go, sir, I demand to see the American consul of the first port at which we touch," said Frank.

"Very well, you can see him, but you can't go ashore. If one goes all must go, and the first thing I know the ship will be deserted. I'll bring the consul aboard to see you."

"That will be perfectly satisfactory, sir. Victory!" whispered Frank to himself as he went up the ladder. "The people triumphant! The ring broken all to smash! A captain cowed in his own cabin by a foremast hand! Hurrah for sailors' rights! We're going to see the consul, Lucas!"

"Aha!" exclaimed the old sailor, with an admiring glance at Frank. "I knew you had the brains,

sir. But I'm sorry we're going to get off so easy.
Me and the rest wanted to see you on that quarter-
deck."

"And a pretty figure I'd make up there, wouldn't
I ?" returned Frank. "I'm glad you didn't have a
chance to carry out your plans."

"What do you think of him, any how ?" asked
the first mate, after Frank had left the cabin.

"I think I've got an elephant on my hands,"
answered the captain. "I don't want to keep him,
and I don't know how to get rid of him. I wish
Billings had been in Guinea before he brought him
aboard here."

"You don't intend to let him see the consul ?"

"Am I as green as that ?" cried the skipper.
"He's got too smooth a tongue in his head and
swings it about too loose and reckless. He and
them two men who were shipped with him must be
kept close while I am ashore after a crew."

"And what will you do with them then ? They
can raise a row with one consul as well as another."

"I know it. Shall I turn them adrift in a boat

or put them on some vessel bound for the States, or set them ashore on some island, and let them shift for themselves?"

"You might transfer them to Gale's boat, and some day when they are off after a whale, clear out and leave them," suggested the third mate. "Gale is a milk-and-water fellow, and not the man at all to get along with a hard crew."

"Well, I must put one of those plans into execution," said the captain, "and circumstances shall decide which it shall be. I am in as great a hurry to see the last of Nelson as he is to see the last of me. I'd knock him overboard if I had a good chance."

"Don't do that, cap'n," said the mate, hastily. "The first one of us who lays an ugly hand on him is booked for Davy's Locker, sure!"

"That's what I am afraid of," said the captain, who being unable to control himself any longer, began to relieve his mind by swearing. "I know how things are going, and besides, Calamity has kept his eyes and ears open."

Two days after this conversation took place between the captain and his mates, the Tycoon dropped her anchor near the spot where the Stranger lay three days afterward. One of the boats was called away at once, a crew selected for her, and the captain started for the shore. Frank felt jubilant when he saw him go off, but Lucas looked rather down-hearted. "He hasn't got a single one of our friends in that boat, sir," said the sailor.

"Of course not," replied Frank. "He wouldn't take them if he knew who they were, for he wants the first chance at the consul himself."

"Yes, and he'll have the last chance too, sir. We'll never see him."

"Very well, if he doesn't bring him off as he promised, I'll jump overboard and swim ashore. I can make the island very easily. You won't pull a boat in pursuit of me."

"No, sir, and nobody else shall. Neither shall the mudhook be hove up till you've had a chance to say a word for us."

"Nelson, the first mate wants to see you in the

cabin," said Mr. Gale, coming forward at this moment. "He is going to offer you something to keep still, and you had better take it."

"If that is all he wants it will be of no use for me to go," answered Frank, "for my mind is made up."

"Go and talk to him, anyhow," said the officer. "Perhaps you can strike some sort of a bargain. I want to see you safe off this craft, and now is your chance, if ever."

"Nelson!" shouted the mate, from the top of the companion ladder.

"Coming, sir," replied Frank.

He went, and was not a little astonished at the reception he met as he entered the cabin. The door was suddenly closed behind him, and before he could think twice he was powerless, his ankles and wrists being heavily ironed. "Not a word out of you," said the first mate, covering Frank's head with a cocked revolver. "You'll find out now who controls this ship—you or her proper officers."

"You ain't as smart as some folks seem to

think," said the second mate, with a grin. " If you were bound to blab, why didn't you take the hundred dollars the cap'n offered you, and wait till you got ashore before you began to swing your chin ?"

Frank made no reply, and could offer no resistance, as the two mates dragged him out of the cabin along a narrow passage-way that led to the hold. They stowed him away among the oil casks and left him to his meditations. This was the way Frank saw the consul at the port of Honolulu.

Having disposed of Frank, the officers made their way back to the cabin, and one of them mounting the companion ladder, called out : " Mr. Gale, tell Lucas that Nelson has got his money, and ask him to come down and get his !"

Lucas came, wondering what arguments the mates had brought to bear upon Frank to work so great a change in his feelings all at once, and when he reached the foot of the ladder he found out what they were—a revolver and a pair of handcuffs. The former held him passive while the irons were slipped on, and then he also was carried to the hold and stowed away, but at such a distance from Frank that the two could hold no conversation. Barton was served in the same manner, and the officers having secured the men of whom they stood the most in fear, breathed freely once more, and told each other that they were still masters of the Tycoon.

The prisoners were kept in the hold almost twelve hours—long enough for the captain to bring his crew of natives on board and get his vessel well out to sea. Then they were released and ordered on deck. Frank was disposed to make the best of his disappointment, knowing that he could not help himself, but Lucas was inclined to smash things. He hunted up his friends as soon as he could—those who had promised to stand by him and Frank through thick and thin—and laid down the law to them in stronger language than we care to quote. "Why, what's the matter?" asked the sailors, as soon as their angry mate gave them a chance to speak. "Where have you been so long?"

" That's what's the matter," replied Lucas, show-ing his wrists.

" That's where I've been so long," he added, tapping the marks the irons had left. " Sailed the blue water, man and boy for thirty-five years, I have, and never had the darbies on me before. Me and Cap'n Nelson's both been there, and Barton too; and here you chaps stood around like so many bumps on a log, and never lifted a· hand to help us !"

" What could we have done, even if we had known that you were in trouble, while the mates were walking around with their pistols strapped to their waists and holding us tight to our work?" asked one of the sailors.

Lucas opened his eyes at this. Did the mates know of the plans that had so often been discussed in the forecastle? It looked like it.

" Somebody's been talking while Calamity was about," said the boatswain's-mate. " Never mind; we've missed one chance, but we'll have better luck next time. The ship's going to Japan, and she'll have another man on her quarter-deck when she comes back."

And so she did, but Lucas did very little toward bringing about the change. It was Captain Barclay himself; but of course he did not intend to do it.

Almost the first man Frank saw when he came on deck after his release was the third mate. "Nelson," said he, earnestly, "I had no hand in this business. If I had known what those men intended to do, I should have warned you."

"I believe you, sir," replied Frank. "I lay nothing to your charge, as you will find when the day of settlement comes."

Frank looked toward the Islands which the ship was fast leaving behind, then at the dusky, muscular Kanakas who thronged the deck, and went to work with a heavy heart. He had already had more than enough of whaling. He did not mind the dangerous, laborious duties he had to perform so much as he did the life he led in the forecastle. Of course it was kept neat and clean, like the rest of the ship,

but it smelled horribly of tar and bilge water, and
the men into whose company he was thrown there,
were not just the sort he would have selected for
associates had he been permitted to choose. It was
bad enough before, but now here were a score and
more of heathen with whom he had to bunk.
Frank did not know how he could stand it. The
only thing that had kept him up thus far was the
belief that all this would end very shortly; but
that hope was gone now, and time only would show
what was in store for him.

Frank worked hard while on duty and talked a
good deal when on watch, to keep himself from
thinking too much. He had the satisfaction of seeing that the captain and his two mates did not treat
the crew with any more severity than they had
always done, and some of the old members of the
ship's company were often heard to declare that
they did not act like the same men. As for the
natives, Frank very soon found reason to change the
opinions he had formed of them. They had all seen
service in whalers, and proved to be the neatest

and most peaceable portion of the crew. More than that, they did not swear, and it was some relief to work by the side of men who could talk without putting an oath or two in every sentence they uttered.

As soon as the ship was fairly under way the mast-head was manned, and the sailors set about preparing themselves for the real business of the voyage. A complete change was made in the boats' crews, and Frank, to his delight, found himself with Lucas, Barton, and two other foremast hands, assigned to the third mate's boat. Frank held his old position as bow-oarsman, and Lucas was boat-steerer. He soon proved himself to be a good one too. He did not fall overboard again, or give Frank any more opportunities to take his place and strike a whale he had missed. During the next three weeks nine whales were added to the stock already in the hold, and of this number four were captured by Mr. Gale's boat. Frank very soon got over his nervousness, and as a consequence went just as far the other way, and was inclined to be a little too daring. He had an uncomfortable habit of wrapping a line about a thwart when he could not hold it, and Lucas, after repeatedly telling him never to do it again, got out of patience, and Frank was moved toward the other end of the boat—"promoted backward." He was seated at the stroke-oar, and the bow-oar given into the hands of Barton, who knew too much of the nature of the game they were hunting to run any risks.

Meanwhile the Tycoon was rapidly approaching her cruising grounds, and one morning the captain told his officers that the Mangrove Islands lay directly in their course two hundred miles distant, and that it was his intention to stop there for water and terrapins. That same day a whale was raised, and the captain and the third mate set off to capture it. The two boats pulled side by side for a mile or more, and then the whale took the alarm and made off. "Never mind, Mr. Gale," shouted the captain. "You keep on after him, and I'll follow you with the ship."

Mr. Gale promptly hoisted his sail and went in

pursuit. The whale led them a long chase, but getting a little over his fright at last, he allowed the boat to approach within striking distance, and gave Lucas a chance to throw his harpoons into him. Then a most terrific fight ensued, which was so long and so stubbornly contested that Frank began to think he had never seen an ugly whale before. The monster seemed determined to destroy his enemies ; but the mate kept at him, and by his excellent management succeeded in taking his boat through the struggle without the loss of any of her crew, and with so little damage that an hour's work by the ship's carpenter would make her fit for sea again. When it was ended and the whale rolled over with his fin out, the mate seized one of the flags, and turned to signal his triumph to the ship.

"It's lucky you wasn't in the bow," said Lucas, drawing his hand across his dripping forehead and nodding to Frank. "If you'd been here with the line wrapped around a thwart when he sounded the last time, there wouldn't have been one of us left to tell the story of this fight!"

"Pass that bucket aft and I'll bail her out," said Frank, drawing a long breath and glad that the danger was over. "He hit us a pretty hard blow with his jaw, and the water is running in here like a small Niagara. What's the matter, Mr. Gale?"

This question was called forth by an exclamation of wonder from the third mate. When he turned to signal the ship he stopped suddenly, looked all around the horizon, and then the flag dropped from his hands. The Tycoon was almost hull down—nothing but her topsails were visible. During the five hours that the brave officer had been pursuing and battling with the whale, the ship was standing away from him instead of coming to his relief, and he had been too busy to see it until this moment.

"What's the matter, sir?" repeated Frank.

Mr. Gale sat down, his face whiter now than it had been at any time during the deadly fight he and his men had just passed through, and pointed toward the Tycoon's receding topsails.

CHAPTER XIII.

TURNED ADRIFT.

FRANK looked, and was not a little surprised to find that the Tycoon, which he had all the while supposed was following the boat, was almost out of sight. He did not understand it at first, but a single glance at the faces of his companions explained it all. Even Lucas, who had shown so much courage a few minutes before, betrayed the utmost consternation now.

"Well, Nelson," said Mr. Gale, in a tone of resignation, "Captain Barclay has got rid of you at last."

"Why, you don't suppose that he intends to desert us!" cried Frank.

The mate shrugged his shoulders and pointed with his thumb toward the ship, as if to say that

16

Frank could see what she was doing as well as he could, and might interpret her actions to suit himself.

" It can't be possible !" said Frank. "No man on earth could be guilty of an act of treachery like this."

" A captain who will allow his men to be abused until they jump overboard to put themselves out of his way, will do anything," returned Mr. Gale, quietly. "Hoist the sail, Lucas ; you had better bail her out, Nelson. We must keep her afloat until she carries us two hundred miles."

" Is there any water, sir ?" asked Barton.

" Yes, the keg is full, and we need a taste of it after our hard work ; but we must touch it lightly, for there is no telling when we shall get any more. The Mangrove Islands are the nearest land, and, as I said, they are two hundred miles away. It is lucky that I know the course."

The sail having been hoisted, the men took a refreshing drink all around, and settled back on their seats to think over their situation. Frank could not yet believe that Captain Barclay had sent them out there alone, with no other object in view than to desert them. He kept telling himself that the ship must have raised another whale and gone in pursuit of it, and he watched her closely, expecting every moment to see her shorten sail and come-to to wait for them; but she kept on, with all her canvas spread, and very soon nothing but her royals were visible above the horizon. Frank was obliged to believe it now, and shuddered when he thought of what was yet to come. With a leaky boat under them, not a mouthful of anything to eat, and with only a very small supply of water to allay the raging thirst caused by their five hours' work under a broiling sun, their situation was one calculated to frighten anybody. But still it might have been worse, and in this thought Frank found a little consolation. The mate knew which way to steer to find land, and if they could only keep the boat afloat twenty-four hours they would be safe. But suppose the boat had been stove during the fight with the whale! Suppose he had cut it in two with his jaw, or smashed it in pieces with his flukes, as he had tried so hard to do, and left the crew struggling in the water: what then! Captain Barclay would have deserted them all the same, and they would have been left powerless. Surrounded by an army of hungry sharks (Frank now and then caught a momentary glimpse of a sharp fin cutting the water as one of these voracious monsters hurried toward the whale they had just left, being attracted no doubt by the blood he had spouted during his flurry), their sufferings would have been ended, and there would have been none left to tell the story of the captain's treachery.

"Come, come, boys! This will never do in the world," said Mr. Gale, suddenly breaking the silence that had reigned for the last half hour. "Wake up, there! What's the matter with you that you look so sober? If we were eight or nine hundred miles out at sea, we'd have something to worry over; but if the wind holds this way, we shall be all right by to-morrow at this time. The Tycoon is going to the Mangrove Islands for water, and maybe we shall be lucky enough to catch her there. If we can't stand it to do without food for that length of time we had better jump overboard at once, for we've no business to be sailors. Come, Lucas, begin there in the bow, and sing a song or tell a story !"

" I can't, sir !" replied the sailor.

" All right. You shan't have any water the next time it is passed around. Go on, Barton. Sing a song or tell a story—a lively one, mind."

" Hold on a bit, sir !" exclaimed Lucas. " I'll do almost anything to get another drink of that water."

This order soon brought about a great change in the feelings of the men. Their minds being diverted from the dangers of their situation, something like merriment soon began to prevail. As it was understood that each one must do his share toward entertaining his companions, and that the first one who failed to tell a story or sing a song when his turn came, should forfeit his next drink of water, this trial of memory and ingenuity was kept up until far in the night. It would seem as though men who had spent their lives amid scenes of danger and excitement could never be at a loss for something to talk about, but even the oldest among the sailors ran short of stories at last, and when this happened they did not hesitate to make up one as they went along; and some of those they told were as ridiculous as the story Dick Lewis told the captain of the fishing boat. Frank drew on his experience among the mountains and in the woods, and his stories must have been worth listening to, for when his turn came the men were all wide awake.

At last when the crew began to show signs of drowsiness, Mr. Gale ordered four of them to make themselves as comfortable as they could and go to sleep, while he and Frank looked out for the boat. Mr. Gale steered by a compass, the face being lighted up by a small lantern with which whale-boats are always provided, and Frank talked to him to keep him awake, and bailed out the water as fast as it ran in. He did not learn anything encouraging during the four hours that he and Mr. Gale kept watch. The mate said they were sure to reach the Islands unless a storm blew them out of

their course or swamped them, but he did not like
to think of the way they would fare after they got
there. The largest of the Islands was often visited
by whalers, he continued, but it was almost a land
unknown. It was a good place to go to get water
and fresh meat in the shape of terrapins, but he
had never yet heard of a boat's crew, who, leaving
the beach to explore the island, had ever returned
to tell what they saw there. Many a fine whale
ship which, when last spoken, had her hold nearly
filled with oil and was almost ready to set out on
her return voyage, had suddenly disappeared, leaving no trace behind. It was supposed that some of
them had gone to the Islands for water, and had
either been wrecked on the treacherous shoals and
reefs with which they were surrounded, or been
captured and plundered by the natives. He had
seen men who had been held captive there for years,
and had only escaped at last by smuggling themselves
on board some vessel whose crew was too strong to
be successfully attacked. But if they succeeded in
getting there they would find an abundance to eat

and plenty of water to drink, and that was better than being tossed about on the waves of the Pacific in an open boat.

Frank now began to understand Captain Barclay's plans. There was more in them than he had at first supposed. The skipper wanted to be rid of Frank and his friends, and the whale they had killed and deserted, furnished him with an excuse for sending the boat away from the ship. When he arrived in port he could say that she had been smashed in pieces by the whale, and all her crew sent to the bottom. He took his chances on this. If the event really happened, so much the better; but if they came through the fight in safety, and succeeded in reaching the Islands, the natives would detain them as prisoners. In either case he was clear of them, and they could never appear against him in a court of justice.

"I can understand all that," said Frank, after he had explained this to the mate, "but there is one thing I can't quite see through: Why did he send you off with us? You never said you would prosecute him, did you? And there are two other men in the boat who never made any threats of that kind. I am very sorry that the friendship you have exhibited for me should have brought you into this trouble. I shall never be able to repay you."

"It wasn't that at all," said the mate, in reply. "The captain has always been afraid of me, and he was just as anxious to get me off the vessel as he was to get you off. I'm not the sort of officer that suits him. I have been a foremast hand myself, and I can't see the beauty of banging men about as if they had no more feeling than so many logs of wood. As for sending these two other men with us, he had to give the boat a full crew, you know, and he put in those against whom he had a grudge."

Frank and the mate talked in this way until almost daylight, and then the former called Lucas and Barton, who steered the boat and kept her bailed out, while Frank and Mr. Gale lay down on the thwarts and slept until the sun grew too warm for them. It was then nine o'clock. As they had no breakfast to serve up they took a drink of water all around, which seemed to aggravate rather than relieve their thirst, the supply the mate allowed them being so small; and at one o'clock by Mr. Gale's watch, when the Mangrove Islands were in plain sight, they emptied the keg.

Propelled by a favorable breeze the boat rapidly approached the land, and finally the outlines of the shore and the trees on the hill-sides could be easily distinguished. Suddenly Mr. Gale arose, and standing erect in the sternsheets, gazed steadily into the little bay toward which the boat was heading. "She's there!" said he, a moment later.

"The Tycoon?" asked Frank, running his eye along the shore in the vain effort to find the object that had attracted the officer's attention.

"Yes, the Tycoon!"

"Will we go aboard of her, Mr. Gale?" asked one of the crew.

"Certainly, just as straight as we can go. We belong to her, don't we?"

The men said nothing in reply, but their actions

told what was passing in their minds. Some seemed delighted, while others beat their open palms with their clenched hands, and banged the oars violently down on the thwarts. It was plain that Captain Barclay had some men in his ship's company who would give him serious trouble if they ever found the opportunity.

"There's something wrong with her," continued the mate, still gazing earnestly at the ship, which Frank had at last been able to discover.

"So I was thinking," said the latter. "She's close in shore and has her topsails aback. She can't be lying-to in there."

"No, she's aground," replied the mate, "and they are trying to work her off."

All eyes were now turned toward the ship which came rapidly into view as the boat approached the shore. It was plain that she was hard and fast aground. The crew were running about the deck, pulling the yards first one way and then the other, in the hope of getting the sails full enough to work her off; but the breeze was not sufficiently strong,

and besides the tide was running out, so that the
ship was every moment sinking more firmly into
her bed on the sand bar. Presently one of the
crew discovered the approaching boat. It was one
of the Kanakas. He gazed at it a moment, then
jumped up and clapped his hands, calling out " Gal-
ickhee !" or some such tongue-twisting name which
he and his people had bestowed upon the third
officer. That brought all the crew to the side, where
they stood waving their hats and shouting out words
of welcome. Frank and the rest were astonished at
this reception. Where were Captain Barclay and
his mates that they permitted the crew to act in this
way ?

" O, Mr. Gale, you're just in time," cried one of
the men, who answered to the name of Boson, " only
I wish you had come a little sooner. We're up to
our necks in trouble."

" Not an officer aboard—all gone—the ship a
thousand miles from water—or she might as well be,
she's so hard a-ground, six men dead and the niggers
thicker than blackberries," chimed in Tully, another

of the crew, stamping about the deck and swinging his arms wildly in the air.

The men in the whaleboat were greatly amazed. They clambered over the side with all possible haste, each one demanding to know what was the matter. The crew shook each of them by the hand as if they were overjoyed to meet them once more, and then silently directed their attention to different parts of the deck, as if telling them to see for themselves what was the matter. Frank stood speechless while he looked. The deck was in the greatest confusion. Harpoons, spades, lances and hand-spikes were scattered about, and with them were mingled curious weapons and ornaments that he had never seen before, and blubber-knives, cutlasses and muskets with the bayonets attached. These last came from the ship's armory, and their presence on deck was enough to prove that there had been a fight, even had other indications been wanting.

A feeble attempt had been made to clear up things a little, but the traces that were left of the recent contest proclaimed that it had been a severe and by no means a bloodless one. Frank ran his eye hastily over the crew gathered about him, and saw that there were some familiar faces missing—among them those of the captain, his two mates and his old enemy, Calamity. What if he had been there when the fight came off? Might not he also have been among the missing? Perhaps Captain Barclay's attempt to get him off his vessel had been the means of saving his life.

" What's been going on here, any how?" demanded the mate, as soon as he could speak.

A chorus of hoarse voices arose in reply, each one trying to give his version of the story, and to make himself heard above his companions; but Mr. Gale, finding that there was nothing to be learned in that way, commanded silence, and pointing to one of the crew ordered him to speak for all. The man complied, telling his story in regular sailor lingo which we put into English as follows :—

The Tycoon arrived at the island that morning about three o'clock, and came to anchor two miles outside the bar. The captain, knowing the treach-

erous character of the natives, kept one watch on
deck until morning, but nothing suspicious being
seen, the ship stood close in at daylight, and came
to; after which the water-barrels were got overboard, and the captain and first mate set out in
their boats to tow them ashore. No sooner had the
crews touched the beach than they were assailed
by a swarm of natives, who had been lying in
ambush waiting for them. Almost at the same
moment two large war canoes filled with savages
made their appearance, coming from one of the
numerous little inlets which set into the land from
the bay. They headed straight for the ship, their
crews brandishing their lances and clubs, and yell-
ing at the top of their lungs.

The sailors on board the Tycoon, who had witnessed the massacre of their shipmates without the
power to aid them, now found themselves called
upon to provide for their own safety. The second
mate, who was in command, made an effort to
bring the ship about and run out of the bay; but
she struck the bar in going around, running on

with sufficient force to knock all the crew off their feet. They could not run, and their only chance for life was to beat off their assailants, who outnumbered them five to one. The weapons that were left in the arm-chest were quickly brought up, muskets, pistols and cartridges to put into them were distributed among the crew, lances, harpoons and spades placed about the deck in convenient nooks, so that they could be readily seized, and by the time these preparations were completed, their foes were upon them. They made the attack at two different points, one canoe running under the bow and the other coming alongside at the starboard quarter. The sailors met them at both places, and the first assault was repulsed. The seamen, having the advantage of position, knocked their assailants over the side as fast as they could climb to the top of the bulwarks, but the natives persevered, and overwhelming numbers began to tell. They succeeded in gaining a footing on deck, and drove the sailors before them toward the waist.

Almost in the beginning of the fight the second

mate had been struck down by a lance, and as there was no one to direct the movements of the sailors, each man fought on his own hook, and did just what he thought best, without paying any attention to his neighbors. Boson probably saved the day. While the sailors were retreating he caught up the mate's revolver, which was lying on deck, and turning fiercely on his foes fired all the barrels in quick succession, every shot striking a native and bringing him dead or wounded to the deck. That was more than the enemy could endure. Appalled by the havoc the six-shooter created, they beat a hasty retreat, followed by the sailors, who thinned their ranks very perceptibly before they could clamber over the side into their boat. As they were about to push off, Boson and Tully added a grand finale to the victory. The former threw a harpoon at one of the natives, which, missing its object, passed through the bottom of the boat, knocking a hole in her that would have caused her to sink long before she could reach the shore, even had Tully not fol-

17

lowed it up, as he did, with the heavy snatch-block,
which made a complete wreck of her.

The enemy being beaten at the quarter, the
sailors who defended that part of the ship ran
to the assistance of their friends in the bow;
but the fight was over there, also. The natives,
failing to gain the deck, became discouraged, and
dropping back into their boat, made all haste to
reach the shore. Some succeeded, others did not.
The sailors rushed for their muskets and pistols,
which they had thrown to the deck after firing their
contents at the foe, and hastily ramming down cartridges, opened fire on the natives. Those of their
companions who were not provided with these
weapons, employed themselves in clearing the deck
of the dead and wounded the savages had left
behind them, tumbling them all unceremoniously
over the side, and never looking to see what became
of them afterward.

The battle being ended, the crew began to look
about them and make an estimate of their losses.
They found that six of their number had fallen

beneath the war-clubs and lances of their assailants, which, counting in the twelve that had gone ashore in the boats, made eighteen men they had lost out of thirty-five. Greatly alarmed, disheartened by the loss of all their officers, and afraid to risk another encounter with their diminished numbers, they hastily committed the bodies of their dead companions to the deep, and set to work to get the ship afloat. They had kept hard at it for more than six hours. They had moved her a little, but the tide began to fall just at the wrong time, and there she was as fast as if she had been nailed to the ground.

The new-comers listened to this story with breathless attention. If any evidence was needed to convince them of its truthfulness, they found it in the frightened faces of the men and the disordered state of the deck, which bore unmistakable signs of the conflict. Their assailants had left some of their property behind them in the shape of lances, war-clubs and head-dresses, and close alongside the ship floated the wreck of the canoe, which was slowly moving out to sea with the tide. A moment later

additional and most unexpected evidence was produced. A warning exclamation uttered by Lucas,
under his breath, drew all eyes toward him. Frank
saw him pick up a lance that happened to be lying
near, and following the direction of his gaze, saw
that it was fastened upon a head which was slowly
rising above the combings of the fore hatch—a head
covered with a mass of shaggy hair. It was one
of the natives, who had no doubt been knocked into
the hold during the fight, and was now coming up
to see if the coast was clear, so that he could make
his escape. Not a man moved. Every one held
his breath as Lucas raised the long, slender whale-
lance in the air and held it poised in both hands.

The head was raised slowly, cautiously, inch by
inch, above the combings of the hatchway, and presently a dark-brown forehead and then a pair of eyes
appeared. At that instant the lance whistled through
the air. Thrown by a practised hand and flying true
to its aim, its keen point was buried in the combings
exactly in range with the spot where the head had
been a second before. Its owner had seen the

weapon coming and dodged just in time, but his escape was a narrow one.

"Avast, there!" cried a voice from the hold. "Ain't you Christians enough to give a white man a chance for life and liberty?"

The sailors stood and looked at one another without speaking.

CHAPTER XIV.

OLD TIMES REVIVED.

I say! on deck, there!" continued the voice. " Don't throw any more of them things at me, and I'll come up!"

These words aroused the crew. They made a rush for the fore-hatch, and when they reached it found the owner of the head crouching among the oil barrels. Frank looked at him in astonishment, and could scarcely believe that he was a white man. His only clothing was a pair of tattered trowsers, and those portions of his person which were un-protected were as brown as sole-leather, made so, no doubt, by long exposure to the sun and weather. Moreover, his body was profusely tattooed, so that at the distance Frank stood from him, he looked as though he had on a tight-fitting under-shirt of some dark-colored material, with light blue slashings.

" Who are you, and where did you come from ?" demanded the mate.

" I'm Chips," replied the man. " I used to be carpenter of the whale-ship Mary Starbuck, that was wrecked here long ago. It was so long ago," he added, putting his hand to his forehead in a bewildered sort of way, " that I have almost forgot how it happened."

" Come on deck," said the mate, in a very different tone of voice, " and tell us all about it."

A dozen pairs of ready hands were stretched down to the prisoner—for such Frank now knew him to be—and in a moment more he was hoisted out of the hold to the deck. Frank had a good view of him then, and saw that he really was a white man. His long, matted beard, which hung down nearly to his waist, had afforded some protection to his breast, and the skin beneath it was almost as white as his own. The man pulled his forelock when he found himself standing in the presence of the mate, and gave his trowsers a regular sailor hitch.

"I remember hearing of the loss of the Starbuck," said Mr. Gale. "The news reached Nantucket just before I sailed; but it wasn't so very long ago—not quite two years."

"Is that all, sir? It seems a longer time to me," said the man, whom we will call by the name he had given. "You're the first white men I've set eyes on since then, except those on the island, and you can't call them white now. Some of them are blacker than I am."

"Do you mean to say that there are men on that island held as prisoners?" asked Frank.

"Four more of 'em, sir, and one has been here, as near as he can calculate, about ten years. I hope you won't sail without trying to do something for 'em, sir. They lead a hard life here."

"How do you happen to be aboard my ship?" asked the mate.

"I came off in one of the canoes, sir, and watching my chance jumped into the hold. I was willing to fight for my liberty, but I was afraid that if I tried to join in with you, you would kill me, not knowing who I was, and if you didn't the natives would, when they saw me trying to desert 'em ; and I was so anxious to see my home and family once more that I didn't dare run any risks."

Chips then went on to tell how he came to be a prisoner in the hands of the islanders. His narrative would make an interesting chapter by itself ; but as it has no bearing on our story, and nothing to do with the events that happened afterward, we condense it into a few sentences. The ship to which he belonged was wrecked while lying at the island to fill up with water. A furious storm first disabled her, so that she could not make an offing, and then drove her high and dry upon the bar. Only two of the crew succeeded in reaching the shore, Chips and another, and they were immediately pounced upon by the natives, who carried them in triumph to their principal village, which was hidden away among the rocky gorges in the interior of the island. They found four other prisoners there, and it was owing to their influence that Chips was so well received. He was a carpenter, and just the man the natives wanted. His companion, however, was nothing but a foremast hand, and not being of any particular use, he was harshly treated, and was often in danger of his life. Being driven desperate at last, he seized the first opportunity for escape that presented itself, and succeeded, at very great risk, in swimming off to a ship that came there for water. He warned the captain off, most likely, for the vessel went away at once, and it was probably through him that the news of the loss of the Mary Starbuck was carried to Nantucket. The five prisoners who were left were constantly on the alert to elude the vigilance of their captors, but this was the first opportunity that Chips had ever found. He and his companions were allowed the freedom of the island until a vessel hove in sight, and then they were hurried to the village and kept under guard as long as she remained.

Being satisfied at last that there was but one way to accomplish his object, Chips made himself perfectly at home on the island, acted quite contented, and finally succeeded in making the natives believe that he had no desire to leave them. He became a savage to all intents and purposes. He took part in their dances and pow-wows, joined in their debates, tried to teach them the use of the fire-arms they found on the vessels that fell into their hands, and so won their confidence that they permitted him to take part in the attack on the Tycoon. Watching his chance, while the fight was in progress, he slipped into the hold, and there he was among his own kind once more.

"And now I hope you'll lend a hand to them poor fellows I left behind, sir," said Chips, in conclusion. "It can be easy done now, but to-morrow it'll be too late. There ain't more'n a hundred fighting men on the island, but to-night they'll send off canoes after help, and in the morning, if you're here, you will have an army of 'em howling about you."

"How far is it to the village?" asked Mr. Gale.

"O, you'll not have to go back to the principal

town, sir," answered Chips. "There's a little fishing village right here on the beach, and the natives will all be there to-night, holding a grand pow-wow and waiting for the help that's coming to-morrow. If we can get close to them and give them a volley before they know it, they'll run like deer!"

"Why I thought you said they had fire-arms," exclaimed the mate.

"So they have, sir, but it would make you laugh to see them use them," said Chips. "They take the butt of a gun under their arms, shut their eyes and turn away their heads before they pull the trigger. They seem to think it is the noise that does the damage. All we want, you understand, sir, is to drive 'em at the start. They won't run far before they'll turn on us, and then they'll fight; but by the time they do that, the prisoners will have had a chance to take care of themselves, and we can be back to our boats. I know just where the village is, and can lead you to it in ten minutes after we touch the beach."

" I suppose you don't know anything about those boats' crews that went ashore ?" said the mate.

"No, sir. Those who were not killed are prisoners, and we'll find them at the village."

The man's proposition was well worth thinking over, the mate told himself. He felt that he had a duty to perform toward the prisoners in the hands of the savages, and he was not the one to shrink from it. True, he had a small force to work with, but if he acted with promptness and decision when the time for action arrived, much might be done. " Boys, turn to and straighten up here," said he, after a moment's reflection. " Let's make the old Tycoon look a little more like herself. Nelson, come with me."

The men went to work with a will—all except Lucas, Barton and Chips, who disappeared in the forecastle for a few minutes. When they came on deck again Chips could hardly have been told from the rest of the crew, his tattooed body being clothed in a full sailor's rig, and his matted hair covered with a new tarpaulin. He lent a hand with the rest, and soon proved that he had not forgotten how to do a seaman's duty.

Frank followed Mr. Gale to the quarter-deck. "What do you think of this?" asked the mate. "Shall we risk it?"

"By all means," answered Frank, quickly. "How would you and I feel if we were held captives by these heathen, and some of our own countrymen should come here, and, after learning our situation, go off without making an effort to help us? We may be able to rescue the captain or some of his men, if they are still alive."

Mr. Gale looked at his companion a little doubtfully.

"O, I mean it," said Frank, who knew what was passing in the officer's mind. "I have no reason to like Captain Barclay, and if I could once bring him before a court of justice he would suffer for what he has done. But this is a different thing. If I get the chance, I'll try just as hard to help him as I would to help you."

"Well, I suppose that is the right sort of feeling."

said the mate, "but it isn't my style, I am free to say. A man who has the heart to turn a boat's crew adrift on the ocean, doesn't deserve any help when he's in difficulty. It's the others I want to work for, but here's the trouble : I don't know anything about this fighting business."

"I've had a little experience in it," said Frank, "and so have Lucas and Barton. They are old men-of-war's men, and I know you can depend on them. I'll give you all the help I can."

"Won't you boss the job ?"

"No, I'd rather not. The men will yield you more prompt obedience."

"I know a story worth two of that, sir. I ain't blind or deaf, either."

After some more conversation it was decided that the Tycoon's crew could not leave the island with clear consciences unless they made some sort of a demonstration in favor of the captives, and Frank was finally prevailed upon to take command of the expedition. This being settled, the first thing the young sailor did was to call Chips aft. He and Mr.

Gale spent an hour in conversation with him, and when the man went forward again Frank held in his hands a map of the island, on which the position of the fishing village, the situation of every hut in it, the shape of the jungle* that surrounded it, and the location of all the paths that led to it were plainly marked. Frank also had a short consultation with Lucas, who, when it was over, made his way forward again, winking and nodding as he always did when he had anything on his mind. His companions tried hard to find out what had passed between him and the captain, as everybody called Frank now; but Lucas, while he seemed to grow in size under the pressure of the secret that had been committed to his keeping, remained as dumb as a tar-buckét.

Everything had now been done that could be done before dark—except getting the boats and weapons in readiness—and Frank recollected that he had been at sea for twenty-four hours in an open boat without anything to eat, and that he was very hungry. Perhaps the savory odors that now and then came

from the galley recalled this fact to his mind. At
any rate they brought his appetite back to him, and
he did ample justice to the abundant meal that was
soon served up. The captain was not there now to
superintend the drawing of the provisions, so the
doctor went into the store-room and helped himself.
The consequence was that some articles which rightfully belonged to the men, but which they had never
tasted since leaving port, such as beans, flour, dried
apples and molasses, found their way into the forecastle. Each man got an extra cup of coffee—
strong coffee, too—an extra tablespoonful of sugar
in it, and all he wanted to eat besides. Mr. Gale
and Frank dined in the cabin and the captain's
steward waited on them.

"That's all right," said Lucas, when the steward
told him of it afterward. "Cap'n Nelson's a cap'n
just as much as Cap'n Barclay, and just as good a
one, too. Don't I know? He belongs in the cabin
and at the head of the table, and he's got to stay there
now. He shan't never come into this forecastle
again!"

18

After dinner two of the boats were overhauled and put in readiness for the expedition, which was to leave the ship as soon as darkness settled down to hide her from the watchful eyes of those on shore, the muskets and pistols were loaded, and a dozen rounds of cartridges provided for each man. Of course these preparations did not escape the notice of the sailors, who knew by them that there was work to be done. It soon got abroad that Frank was at the head of the affair, and that set Lucas and Barton in ecstacies. This made them think of old times; and so eager were they for the fight, that they almost got up a row with Boson and Tully just to get their hands in. They did not neglect, too, to make sundry little arrangements with their companions in regard to the treatment the captain and first mate were to receive in case they were found among the prisoners. They would do their best to rescue the friends of Chips, but Captain Barclay should not come back to the ship, no matter what happened. All this, however, was upset by a simple order from their wide-awake leader, who seemed to see everything, know everything and who neglected nothing.

The boats and weapons being in readiness, all the crew were ordered below to rest and sleep, except a boat-steerer's watch, who remained on deck to look out for the ship. Even these were permitted to lie down on deck, with the exception of one man, whose duty it was to keep an eye on the shore, and report anything suspicious that he might see going on there.

The men were allowed to sleep until nine o'clock, when they were called on deck to prepare for action. An abundant and well-cooked supper was served up and eagerly devoured by the grateful foremast hands, who told one another that if Captain Nelson and Mr. Gale were the officers of the ship, they'd never have any trouble with their crew, but they wouldn't catch much grease. They'd feed their men so high that they would get too fat to see a spout or pull an oar.

Supper over, the men were mustered on the quarter-deck to listen to Frank's plan of the campaign. He had made up his mind what ought to be done and assigned each man a particular duty, giving him his orders so plainly that there was no possible chance for a misunderstanding. One order was, that every hut in the village was to be set on fire—they wanted a light to fight by—but it must first be searched to make sure that it contained no prisoners. Some of the boats' crews might be bound or severely wounded and unable to help themselves; and such unfortunates needed especial care and must be looked after by trustworthy men. If any wounded were discovered, they must be turned over to Lucas and Barton, who would assist them back to the boats and remain there to guard them. The men thus designated raised their hands to their caps and said, "Ay, ay, sir!" but when Frank turned to another sailor to give him his orders, they looked at each other and scowled fiercely.

"Now here's a go," muttered Barton. "Suppose we find the first mate with a lance or something through his leg! Eh?"

"Or the cap'n," whispered Lucas, in great disgust.

"Must we bring him to the boat, carry him like he was a blessed little baby, and then watch to see that the niggers don't slip around and send him to Davy's Locker, where he belongs?" added Barton.

"Them's the orders."

"I don't care. I won't do it."

"Avast, there! Better not go agin orders when they come from *him*," whispered Lucas, jerking his thumb towards Frank. "Besides, didn't he say we was men as could be trusted?"

"Ay, so he did," answered Barton, after thinking a moment. "So he did. We can't go back on him after that."

Having given his instructions in the plainest language he was master of, Frank went back to the head of the line and made each man repeat what he had said to him, to make sure that he fully understood what was required, and then he distributed the weapons and ammunition. The Kanakas, although as eager for the fight as their white companions, declined to accept the muskets that were

offered them, preferring to use the lances and war-
clubs the natives had left behind them. It was a
motley-looking company altogether, Frank told himself, after they were all armed and stood awaiting
his orders—very unlike the well-provided and well-
disciplined blue jackets he had been accustomed to
command on expeditions similar to this.

Everything being in readiness, Frank nodded to
Mr. Gale, who ordered the boats to be lowered away
and the crews to tumble into them. Frank took
every man, knowing that the natives would not
attack the ship while their homes were in danger.
When every one was in his place he clambered down
into one of the boats, Mr. Gale having charge of
the other, and led the way toward the beach. Ar-
riving within a few rods of it the boats were brought
to a stand still, and Chips slipped noiselessly into
the water and struck out for the beach, accompanied
by Lucas, who carried a blubber-knife between his
teeth. Chips might have been astonished to know
that Lucas had orders to use the blubber-knife at the
very first sign of treachery. This was the secret

the old boatswain's mate had been carrying all the afternoon. Frank believed the story Chips had told him, but he was so wary that he neglected no precautions to insure the success of the expedition and the safety of the men composing it.

At the end of half an hour the two men made their appearance again, coming alongside so silently that Frank did not see them until they laid hold of the gunwale. They reported the coast clear. The natives, not dreaming of danger, were all at the village, going through some sort of a ceremony intended to bring them success in the next attack they made on the ship, and which Chips said would not be delayed longer than daylight. Frank breathed easier now. Chips was not trying to lead him into an ambush, and that was one thing off his mind.

Slowly and noiselessly the boats approached the shore, and when their bows touched the sand the crews disembarked. The two men selected to guard them promptly took their positions, and the rest fell in behind Chips, who led them along a narrow path through darkness so intense that Frank, who followed close at his heels, was obliged to take hold of his clothing in order to keep track of him. Ten minutes' walk brought them within sight of a bright fire, which they could see shining through the trees in front of them. There they stopped. Frank whispered to the men as they came up óne after another, showed them the position of the village, and they lost no time in taking up the positions he assigned them. When they had all moved off to the right and left, Frank, Mr. Gale and Chips were left alone. They waited and listened for a few minutes, and then moved down the path until they obtained a view of the fire. It was a large one, and threw out so much light that every hut in the village could be distinctly seen. There were about two hundred of the natives in sight, men, women and children, and some were seated in a circle about the fire, while others stood erect, looking intently toward the jungle where Frank knew the right of his line was taking up its position. Their quick ears warned them of the approach of an enemy.

At this moment Frank caught the gleam of a bayonet on the extreme left of the line. That told him that some of his men were in position, and he decided to begin operations at once. He nodded to his companions, and instantly three muskets were levelled and belched forth their contents in quick succession. This was the signal for the attack, and it was promptly obeyed. Muskets and pistols roared all along the line, and such a chorus of hoarse voices arose from the jungle that Frank, had he not known just how many men he had at his command, would have supposed that there was a small army hidden there.

The natives behaved just as Chips said they would. The most of them took to their heels at once, while the bravest among them lingered long enough to fire their muskets. But they discharged them any how—just as they happened to pick them up—and Frank saw that the muzzles of the most of them were pointed into the air. No sooner were the weapons emptied than the owners threw them down and ran for life.

In two minutes' time the sailors were all in the now deserted village, and two of the huts had been fired by Chips, who showed himself as active as a cat. He ran about with a fire-brand in each hand, calling loudly on the captives to make all haste to reach the beach, telling them they would find boats there and men to protect them.

Frank remained in the centre of the line, so that he could see all that was going on and direct the movements of his men, and it was with no little satisfaction that he noted the care with which each member of his small company took to carry out the instructions given him. Frank did not see that any of the natives were killed, but he did see one prisoner rescued. He did not get a glimpse of his face or of his clothing, but a remark Lucas made as he and Barton carried him by in their arms, told him who it was. " This ain't such a nice piece of business as it might be, sir," said the former, touching his cap.

" It's the captain," thought Frank. " That was a lucky thought of mine, appointing two of his worst enemies to take care of him, for they wouldn't injure him now for the world. He's badly hurt, too. Will he act more like a man now, or be a worse tyrant than ever?"

In a very short space of time the whole village was in a blaze. The huts being built of bamboo and their cone-shaped roofs thatched with dry grass, they burned like so much tinder. There was nothing more to be done now—nothing more they could do. They had rescued one prisoner, given the others a chance to run if they were able to do it, and now he must take care of his own men before the natives turned on them. The signal to retreat, a long, shrill whistle, was as promptly obeyed as the signal to attack. The men hurried toward him, and throwing their weapons on their shoulders fell in behind Chips, who led the way toward the beach at a dog trot. Frank ran his eye over the line as it moved passed him to see if there was anybody missing, and found to his delight that not only were the men all there, but also two more rescued prisoners, the captain's harpooner and bow-oarsman, who saluted him as they went by. When the last man was in the path, Frank and Mr. Gale fell in and brought up the rear. A few minutes' rapid run brought them to the beach, and after seeing the wounded captain stowed away as comfortably as circumstances would permit, Frank ordered the crews into the boats, which were pushed off toward the ship. There was no pursuit attempted, the natives being too badly frightened to rally immediately. By the time their expected reinforcements arrived, the Tycoon was safe out of their reach.

CHAPTER XV.

FRANK ON THE QUARTER-DECK.

THE expedition was ended and well ended too, Frank told himself. Three men were rescued, and that was something to feel glad over. The attack was so well planned, and all the details carried out so faithfully and energetically, that it was entirely successful, and there was not a man missing. All the ship's company could be accounted for except Gardner—Frank could not bring himself now to think of him by the name he generally bore —and he had doubtless been killed and thrown overboard when the natives made their attack on the vessel.

While on the way back to the Tycoon Frank had much to think about, the principal object of his thoughts being the wounded captain. Frank was sorry to see him in his present situation, and he reproached himself when he reflected that he had so long cherished feelings of revenge toward him. He had all the while told himself that his feelings were not actuated by any desire for vengeance—that he wanted to have the skipper shut up for a while, merely to prevent him from serving others as he had served himself; but now he knew that behind all this was the belief that the captain deserved punishment for the offences of which he had been guilty, and that he would breathe a good deal easier if he could assist in bringing it about. That was all past now, however. The skipper needed assistance, and that was enough for the generous Frank, who felt almost as tender toward him as he would have felt toward his cousin Archie, had he been in the same situation.

Meanwhile an animated conversation was going on between Mr. Gale and Lucas, who were in the other boat with Barton, the coxswain. The third mate had been silent and thoughtful for a long time, and Lucas asked the reason for it.

"I was just thinking of what's to come," replied Mr. Gale. "Here we have been risking our lives to free these men, and what are we going to do with them now that we have got them?"

"Take them aboard the ship, sir," said Lucas.

"And what's to be done with the ship? The cap'n is of no use now, the first and second mates are gone, and so, of course, the ship falls to my hands; but she's a bigger load than I can carry."

"Don't worry about that, sir," returned Lucas, quickly. "Cap'n Nelson's shoulders are broad, and he can carry her."

"Was he ever master of a vessel?" asked Mr. Gale.

"Of course he was, sir. Didn't you know it?"

"I heard something about it, but I didn't believe it. He don't look like a sailor."

"No more'n he looks like a lawyer or a fighting man, sir; but he's all three. When the war was going he commanded as fine a brig as ever sailed in Farragut's fleet."

"A brig!" echoed Barton. "A ship, you mean.

Haven't I seen her often? Didn't I see her and him too down there in Mobile Bay, the time we had the fight with the forts and gunboats? You're right I did. The Admiral was going to put him in command of a frigate, only the war closed and Cap'n Nelson wouldn't stay in the navy."

"I knew it was something of that kind," said Lucas, who knew just nothing at all about it. He and Barton were working to put Frank on the Tycoon's quarter-deck, and they did not care how many falsehoods they told or what means they used to get him there. "He went into a fight once and licked the rebels three to one," continued Lucas.

"Five to one, you mean," corrected Barton, who did not think his friend was saying quite as much as could be said in Frank's favor.

"I knew it was big odds," returned Lucas, "and under them circumstances, sir, you mustn't feel hard if we say that we won't serve on the Tycoon under nobody but Cap'n Nelson."

"I don't feel hard toward you," said the mate,

"for I don't want to command her. I am not fit."

"No more you be, sir," said Barton, bluntly; "but Cap'n Nelson is. We can call him cap'n now, and nobody can't say no to us without getting his head broke."

Frank, little dreaming of what was passing in the other boat, was being carried rapidly ahead by the stalwart Kanakas who pulled him, and reached the ship a long distance in advance of Mr. Gale. As he came alongside he saw two men looking over the rail, both of whom Chips recognised, dark as it was. They proved to be two wrecked sailors who had been held prisoners by the natives, and who had taken advantage of the attack on the village to run to the beach and swim off to the vessel. They were overjoyed to find themselves among their own countrymen once more, and almost overwhelmed Frank by their exhibition of gratitude. But he had no time to listen to them. He simply shook hands with them, and then turned his attention to the captain.

19

The wounded man groaned whenever any one touched him ; but a whip being quickly rigged he was hoisted aboard as tenderly as possible, and in obedience to Frank's directions was carried into the cabin and placed in his bunk. When the steward lighted the lamp Frank had a good view of him for the first time, and he could hardly bring himself to believe that this wreck of humanity was the same man he had so often seen on the quarter-deck. He was no surgeon, but knowing that something ought to be done at once to relieve the captain and stop the flow of blood, he set to work to do what he could. He cut off the sufferer's coat and shirt with his knife, and found three gaping wounds, which were enough to have left the life out of any but a man of iron, as the captain was. While he was bathing them with warm water brought from the galley the third mate came in, and Frank was surprised to see him remove his hat.

" Is it necessary for me to apologize for coming in here under such circumstances as these, without an invitation ?" asked the amateur doctor.

" I guess not, sir," answered the officer, with a smile. " From all I can learn you've got the best right here."

" How is that? I don't understand you."

" Why, the men have put you in as cap'n, and say they won't do duty under anybody else."

" Well, they have no right to do anything of the kind. They don't know what they are talking about."

" No, they don't. I'm master of this ship," murmured the wounded man, looking about with the old savage glare in his eyes and trying to raise his head. " Trice 'em all up, and hang the snatch-block to their—Mr. Gale!" he ejaculated, recognising the third mate.

" Yes, sir; it's Mr. Gale, come back safe and sound, and just as ready to do duty as he was before you turned him adrift in that boat," replied the officer.

" Send the first mate here," said the captain, sinking back on his pillow and closing his eyes.

" I can't, sir. He went ashore with you and

hasn't come back yet. The natives made an end
of him, most likely."

"The second mate, then."

"Can't send him either, sir, because he and the
first are keeping company now somewhere besides
on board this ship. The natives harpooned him.
There's nobody left but me."

"And you ain't worth nothing. You don't know
how to flog a man."

"If I did, I couldn't do it now, sir. The men
have taken the ship and put Cap'n Nelson in command. I looked for 'em to do it long ago."

"Nelson!" groaned the captain, opening his eyes
again. "I sent him——"

He seemed to recognise the face bending over
him, and stopped suddenly.

"I know you did, sir," said Mr. Gale, "You
sent him adrift with me; but he's back again, and
so are Lucas and Barton and all the rest of the
boat's crew. But I say, cap'n, if you are able to
do duty, you'd best be giving some orders, for the

tide is about turning, and if the ship is to be worked off the bar, now's the time."

The captain made no reply, and neither could Mr. Gale induce him to speak again. He lay with his eyes closed, and groaned every time a question was asked him. The mate scratched his head in great perplexity. "What shall I do, sir?" said he, looking at Frank.

"Do just what you think best," was the reply. "This man is in no condition to give orders. Go ahead on your own hook."

The mate clapped his hat on his head and hurried up the ladder. He found the crew gathered in the waist waiting, no doubt, to hear from some one in the cabin. "Turn to, lads," said Mr. Gale, briskly. "Bear a hand, and get up that small kedge for'ard."

"Who give them orders, sir, begging your pardon for being curious?" said Lucas. "Did Cap'n Barclay or Cap'n Nelson?"

"Cap'n Nelson," replied the mate. "Cap'n Barclay ain't fit to command now."

"No more was he ever fit to command, sir!" said Lucas, who was speaking for all of the men. "But, asking your pardon again, sir, I'd just like to have a peep at Cap'n Nelson, and see why he don't come up and give his own orders, like the master of a ship had ought to do. You know that he went into that cabin once and didn't come out again very soon, don't you? We don't think as much of you, by no means, as we did before you had a hand in that business."

The mate made no reply. He had set himself right with Frank, who was perfectly satisfied that he was not to blame for anything that had happened, and he would leave him to make the matter straight with the men. He stepped aside to allow Lucas to pass, and the latter, running down the companion-ladder, was amazed to find Frank acting the part of Good Samaritan to one whom he had hitherto regarded as an enemy. He opened his eyes wide at the sight, aud Frank thought he was displeased. "It's all time wasted, sir," said he.

"Well, we must do the very best we can for

him," was Frank's reply. "If he can only hold out till we fall in with some ship carrying a surgeon, he will perhaps pull through all right."

"Did you give orders to have the ship worked off the bar, cap'n?" asked the boatswain's mate.

"We want to get her off, don't we?" answered Frank. "She musn't lie here and be pounded to pieces, as she will be if the wind rises."

Lucas went out of the cabin satisfied. He knew what ought to be done as well as anybody, but he wanted to be sure that the orders came from the right source. The men were satisfied too, and went to work to get the ship out of her dangerous situation, while Frank kept busy with his patient, although he believed, with Lucas, that his efforts to save the captain's life would be useless. He had nothing to work with—no lint or bandages, and no medicine to allay the fever. But the sequel proved that Frank did not know what the old sailor meant by his remark. The wounded skipper was threatened by another danger from which no one on board the

Tycoon but Frank could protect him—the fury of
the men he had wronged.

At the end of two hours the Tycoon was in deep
water and standing away from the inhospitable Islands with all her canvas spread. Frank had been
equally successful with the work to which he had
devoted himself, and now the captain was in a sound
sleep. While Frank stood watching him, wondering what was to be done when he awoke, since there
were no medicines aboard except calomel and salts,
nothing to eat except coarse ship's fare, and nothing to drink but the miserable stuff called tea and
coffee which the cook served up twice each day
—while Frank was thinking about this, and wish-
ing he could get inside the Stranger's pantry long
enough to secure some of the delicacies he knew to be
stowed away there, he was aroused by a great hubbub which suddenly arose on deck. He heard the
stamping of feet and loud yells of triumph, mingled
with cries of, " Here's one of 'em. Pitch him
overboard !" A moment later the mate's voice was
heard in tones of remonstrance, to which some one

replied : " If you don't go aft where you belong and mind your own business, you'll go over too !"

Mr. Gale evidently thought that the man, who-ever he was that said this, was in earnest, for Frank heard him running along the deck, and saw his pale face appear at the top of the companion ladder. " Come up, cap'n," he cried, in great excitement; " the men are going to throw Calamity overboard !"

Frank lingered just long enough to slap his pockets, to make sure that the pistols he had carried during the attack on the village were still there, and then went up the stairs in three jumps. He saw a group of men in the waist, who were pushing and crowding one another about, and caught just one glimpse of the pale face of Gardner, who was in the midst of them, and resisting to the utmost the efforts that were being made to drag him to the side. He saw at a glance that Boson and Tully were the ringleaders, and the ones who had seized the fright-ened man ; and he was sorry to see, too, that Lucas and Barton were there and making no effort to restrain their companions, although they took no part in the proceeding. The peaceable Kanakas were standing in a body on the forecastle and looking on in great amazement.

With three jumps more Frank was in the waist, standing between the men and the rail, and Mr. Gale was at his side. "Lucas! Barton!" he cried, "come over to this side the deck."

"Why, cap'n?" began Lucas.

"No words," interrupted Frank. "You and Barton come over to this side of the deck, and be quick about it."

The sailors obeyed, and the change in their positions seemed to make a corresponding change in their feelings, for the next order Frank gave was responded to without an instant's hesitation. "Lucas, take hold of Boson. Barton, grab Tully and drag him away. Gardner, go into the cabin!"

It was wonderful how quickly and easily one calm, determined spirit controlled those angry men. The trouble was ended at once. Boson let go his hold and slunk away at the sight of Lucas's big fist, which was brandished before his eyes, and Tully was equally active in giving ground before the broad-shouldered Barton. Gardner, finding himself at liberty, went down the companion-ladder like a flash, banging the door behind him.

"I am surprised at you, men," said Frank, sternly, and there was not one among them who could look him in the eye. "If you had succeeded in accomplishing your object, what would you have said for yourselves when you got ashore? Boson, you are the largest and strongest man in the crew. Take your stand at the top of that ladder and knock the first one down who attempts to go into the cabin without Mr. Gale's permission."

This stroke of policy on Frank's part won him a fast friend on the spot—one who might otherwise have been an enemy, and kept the crew in a constant uproar. He was a turbulent fellow, this Boson, and one of the few sailors Frank had met who seemed to need a handspike or belaying-pin over his head about once a day to keep him in order. His appearance was enough to frighten some men, and was a good index of his character. He had a most repulsive countenance, a small bullet-shaped head, always kept closely cropped and set on a thick, muscular neck, and a form betokening immense physical power. And indeed he possessed it. He could handle an eighteen-foot oar as if it were a feather, and when he laid out his strength, he fairly made things snap. His whole body was seamed and scarred by wounds he had received in fights and from the officers he had sailed under, and Frank had seen him knocked flat with a handspike which seemed to make no more impression on his thick skull than it would on the mast. This was the man of whom Frank had been wise enough to make a friend.

Boson looked at him in amazement, evidently at a loss to decide whether Frank was in earnest or not; but making up his mind at last that he was, he marched off, and taking the position assigned him, looked defiantly at the crew, as if daring them to come on.

Frank was surprised at the ease with which the disturbance had been quelled, and so was Mr. Gale.

It leaked out afterward that the former's prompt action had prevented serious trouble. Lucas made no idle threat when he said that the captain and Calamity were both to go overboard. The latter had been hiding in the hold among the oil barrels. He went there when he saw the natives approaching to make their attack on the ship, and no one missed him until the fight was over, and the sailors began to look around to see how many they had lost. Not finding Calamity among the slain, they concluded that he had either jumped overboard, or been wounded and thrown over; but he had been safely concealed in the hold all the while. Finding at last that the ship was in motion, he came out of his hiding-place to see what was going on, and must have been astonished at the reception extended to him. After he had been disposed of, the skipper's turn was to come next. The desperate men counted on meeting with opposition and perhaps resistance from Mr. Gale and Frank, but expected to overcome it very easily. They knew Mr. Gale, but found they did not know Frank. Had the latter been as easily cowed as the third mate was, something certainly would have happened.

Quiet being restored, Mr. Gale and Frank walked aft together, and the crew seeing them in earnest conversation, leaned over the rail and waited to learn what would come next. "I suppose the first business is to decide who we want for officers," said Frank.

"I suppose so, sir," replied Mr. Gale.

"You are entitled to the captain's berth, of course. That's settled."

"No it ain't, sir," returned the mate, quickly. "This is the first voyage I ever made as an officer, and I know no more about navigation than I do about the moon."

"Then let me act as your sailing-master."

"The men won't agree to it, sir. They said so."

Then the mate went on to repeat the conversation that had taken place between Lucas, Barton and himself, at which Frank laughed heartily. "Why they are very much mistaken," said he. "The largest sailing vessel I ever commanded was a pleasure yacht."

"No odds, sir. They've got it in their heads that you must command them now that the old man is done for, and there'll be a row if you don't. You have seen what they are when they get started."

"Then I'll tell you what we'll do," said Frank, after thinking a moment. "We'll leave it to them; and after they have selected their officers we'll draw up a paper containing a full history of everything that has happened since leaving Honolulu, and ask them to sign it. These matters must be looked into by the consul, and we want to be all right in law, you know."

In accordance with this suggestion, the mate mustered the men on the quarter-deck and made them a little speech. He told them that there must be somebody at the head of affairs, and that as the officers were all gone except himself, others must be selected. In the first place they must all agree to be bound by the decision of the majority, and faithfully promise to obey those placed over them.

"We'll all obey Cap'n Nelson," exclaimed Boson, before the mate was fairly done speaking.

"Yes, Cap'n Nelson! Cap'n Nelson!" cried a chorus of hoarse voices. "Nobody else!"

There was not a dissenting voice; so Frank could no longer refuse to accept the responsibility. He was amused to see that Lucas and Barton, while supporting Boson's nomination, looked savagely at him, as if they would have been glad to knock him down for speaking in such a hurry. They wanted to bring Frank forward themselves.

"Cap'n Nelson, I give place to you, sir," said Mr. Gale.

The men greeted the young commander with cheers as he stepped forward, no doubt expecting him to make them a speech; but Frank did nothing of the kind. He told them that the next business was to select a first mate, and at his suggestion Mr. Gale was chosen by a unanimous vote. Lucas was put in for second, and Boson, who was a fine sailor,

FRANK CHOSEN CAPTAIN OF THE TYCOON.

if he was a quarrelsome fellow, for third mate ; and when the men were dismissed every one of them seemed satisfied.

Frank at once went below to look at his patient, leaving Mr. Gale in charge of the deck. The captain lay with his eyes closed, rolling his head from side to side, and Calamity was fanning him with his hat. The latter started up in alarm as Frank entered.

"It is no one who is going to harm you," said he. "I hope you see now what you have brought upon yourself by your way of doing business. Let it be a lesson to you."

"I shall never dare to go into the forecastle again," whined Calamity.

"You needn't go in there. You will stay here as the captain's nurse."

This order seemed to relieve the frightened man. Through the open skylights he had heard all that passed on deck, and he was afraid that Frank, having the authority to do so, would order him to go forward where he belonged.

20

Frank slept but little that night. The responsibilities of his new position weighed on his mind, and he came on deck every hour to see that things were going straight. The first real duty he performed as captain was to ascertain whereabouts in the wide world the ship was, and this he did the next day by an observation. She was directly in the track of vessels bound from Australia to the Pacific ports of the United States, and he decided to cruise about for a few days in the hope of meeting some ship that carried a surgeon. Without medical assistance he was afraid that the captain might not live until the ship reached Honolulu, which, according to his calculations, was more than fifteen hundred miles distant.

The observation made, dinner over and the table cleared away, Frank busied himself for an hour or two in drawing up papers for the men to sign; and when that was done, he took a few minutes to think over the various incidents that had operated to place him in his present position. The most exacting old sea-dog could hardly have found fault with the way affairs were going now. The weather-side of the quarter-deck was reserved for the captain, who for an hour paced up and down there with his hands behind his back, and as free from intrusion as a monarch on his throne. The officers were alert and watchful, the crew seemed to have settled down to the new order of things as if they had been accustomed to them all their lives, and never in her best days under her old commander had the Tycoon looked more ship-shape. Frank wished the crew had put Mr. Gale in his place, and left him to act as sailing-master; but since they had seen fit to do differently, he would perform his duty as best he could. He knew every rope and sail in the ship, was possessed of excellent judgment, which was the one great thing needed, and the captain's sextant came as handy to him as a fishing-rod or double-barrel; so he was not so very unfit for the position he held after all. How Archie and the rest of the friends he had left on the Stranger would open their eyes if they could see him in that dress and know that he was the master of that fine ship! For the first time in a long while Frank allowed his thoughts to wander back to them, and the consequence was he became homesick. Yes, homesick; for the cabin of the Stranger had been his home for almost eight months, and had he kept out of the way of the bogus captain, it might have been his home yet. Where was the schooner now, and what were those aboard of her doing? Perhaps she was sailing about over the Pacific in search of the Tycoon! This thought aroused Frank from his reverie, and caused him to straighten up and look about as if he expected to see something. If the Stranger followed the Tycoon to the Sandwich Islands, would not Uncle Dick ascertain when he got there that she had shipped a crew and started for the Japan station? And would he not sail again immediately and try to find her?

"Sail ho!" shouted the man at the masthead. "Where away?" demanded the captain, greatly excited.

"Two points off the lee bow, sir. Steamer."

"Dear me ! why did he say steamer ?" thought Frank. "I'd rather he'd have said topsail schooner."

No doubt he would, especially if the schooner proved to be the Stranger. Still he was glad to know that there was a steamer near, for he would be relieved of one cause of anxiety if he could only intercept her. He would bring her doctor aboard, and perhaps he could do something for the captain.

CHAPTER XVI

CONCLUSION.

FRANK went aloft with his glass, and after watching the steamer for a few minutes made up his mind that if he held on his way she would cross his path at such a distance that he could not speak her; so he altered the Tycoon's course a few points, and for several miles ran almost parallel with the approaching craft. This manœuvre was successful, and by sunset the two vessels were within hailing distance. After seeing one of the boats cleared for lowering and the crew ready to tumble into her, Frank came to while the steamer was yet a half a mile away; and this attracting the attention of her captain, he ran under a slow bell until within speaking distance, when he stopped his engines. His vessel was a fine large mail steamer, and her promenade deck was crowded with passengers.

"Steamer ahoy!" yelled Frank, through his trumpet. "Will you wait for me to send a boat aboard of you? We are in need of medical assistance."

A reply in the affirmative promptly came back, and five minutes afterward a whale-boat, manned by a sturdy crew steered by Frank, was pulling toward the steamer.

Up to this time Frank's mind was fully occupied with thoughts of the wounded captain; but now it occurred to him that he was not in just the right dress to present himself before a company of ladies and gentlemen. Clothed in a red shirt, coarse trowsers, heavy boots, all plentifully spattered with oil, a tarpaulin, which, although but a short time out of the slop-chest, began to show signs of wear, and with hands and face browned by exposure, he was not the most attractive looking young man in the world, and he thought he looked worse when in the presence of the dapper young officer who met him at the gangway. The well-dressed people on deck gave him plenty of room as he walked along, but the gray-headed captain came forward and greeted him cordially. "What did you say you wanted, sir?" said he. "A doctor?"

"Yes, sir. There's a man aboard that ship in a critical condition. We had some trouble with the natives at the Mangrove Islands, and he's badly wounded."

A chorus of ejaculations and questions arose from the passengers who crowded eagerly forward, and Frank could have told his story to a most attentive and interested audience if he had only had time; but the captain sent off at once for the surgeon, who made his appearance before he was fairly begun. To him Frank described the nature of the captain's injuries as well as he could, and when he had heard all Frank could tell him, he provided himself with medicine and instruments, got into the whale-boat and was taken on board the Tycoon. He remained there nearly three hours—so long that some of the gentlemen among the steamer's passengers became impatient at the delay, called on Frank for a boat, and came off to see what the "blubber-hunter" looked like. The young captain met them as they came over the side, and was amused at the look of astonishment that settled on their faces when they found themselves fairly on her deck.

"Why, if I had known that you kept your craft as neat as this, I should have brought my wife and daughter along," said one of the gentlemen, running his finger over the rail and closely examining it to make sure that there was no oil on it. "I expected to find myself knee-deep in grease. I have seen whalers come into port before now, and they were such horrible looking things outside, that I supposed. they could not be very tidy on deck."

"They are not always, sir," said Frank, "especially when they are cutting in and trying out. They often spend eight months and more out of sight of land, and the men are so busy with other work that they can't find time to keep the ship as neat and trim as a merchantman or man-of-war."

The visitors having satisfied themselves that they

were in no danger of soiling their good clothes, began to exhibit a lively interest in what they saw about them. Frank showed them over the ship, explained the use of the try-works, harpoons, lances and all the other implements connected with a whaler's calling, and related the particulars of the fight they had had with the natives at the Mangrove Islands; and so engrossed did his listeners become that they were sorry when the doctor came out of the cabin and announced that he was ready to depart. He told Frank what he had done for the wounded man, and said that, although he was so badly used up that it might take him some months to fully recover from the effects of his injuries, there were no bones broken, and his life was in no danger, if the remedies he left for him were faithfully administered according to the directions he had given the captain's attendant. The doctor and the passengers were then taken on board their vessel by one of the whale-boats, and when it returned and was hoisted at the davits, the Tycoon filled away for the Sandwich Islands.

It was wonderful what a change the doctor's visit made in the wounded man! He seemed to grow better immediately. Frank found him in earnest conversation with Calamity. When it was ended the latter came out with the request that Mr. Gale might be sent to the captain when he was off duty, if Frank had no objection. Of course he had none. The first mate was sent for at once, and remained in conversation with the captain for more than an hour. When he came · out he went straight to Frank, who was pacing the quarter-deck. "How is he now?" asked the latter.

"O, he's all right that is, his tongue is as lively as ever. He wants me to act as mediator between you and him."

"There is no occasion for it," answered Frank. "There are no hard feelings on my part."

"I was sure of it, sir. Calamity has told him everything, and he would be perfectly satisfied with the way matters have been arranged, if it wasn't for the fear that you helped rescue him from the natives, and brought the doctor off to save his life, so that you might have the chance to take him before the court at Honolulu."

"Perhaps if he knew me better he would not have so poor an opinion of me," returned Frank. "I don't deny that if I could have got him there two days ago, I should have made trouble for him. Indeed I told him so to his face. But that is all over now."

"He has been punished enough, hasn't he, sir?"

"I think he has. You may assure him for me, in the plainest language you can command, that I shall not trouble him in any way. On the contrary, I will do what I can to make him comfortable."

"I'll tell him, sir. He wanted me to ask two favors of you: one is, that you will put him on board the first ship you meet bound for the States. He's afraid of the men, sir. Calamity told him that they were going to throw him overboard."

"He has nothing to fear from them, but I'll respect his wishes all the same. What else does he want me to do?"

"He hopes that while you are looking out for a sail,

you will keep an eye open for whales and lose no chance for filling up. We stow twenty-five hundred barrels, and here we have been out nearly seventeen months and haven't taken a quarter of that quantity. It looks now as though we were not going to make a paying voyage."

"I'll do the best I can," replied Frank.

And he did. The ship lay-to that night with only a boat-steerer's watch on deck, and the next morning business began in earnest. A whale was discovered before breakfast, and three boats in command of Mr. Gale, Lucas and Boson were sent out after him, Frank remaining in charge of the ship. The prize was secured without much trouble, and while it was lying alongside, and the men, having prepared themselves for work by eating a good breakfast, were about to begin the cutting in, another was raised, and by three o'clock that also was alongside, and the carpenter was at work on a stove boat. This whale fought hard, but there was nobody hurt.

This was only the beginning. The blubber-room

was never entirely empty, and during the next three weeks four hundred barrels of oil were added to those in the hold. Of course the labor was severe, the crew being small, but the men had plenty to eat, were kindly treated and the amount of work they turned off was surprising. Calamity kept the captain posted in all that was going on, and he growled lustily—being an old sailor he couldn't help it—and wondered why he had not been blessed with such luck, and why the crew had not worked as well for him as they did for the new captain.

One bright morning, following a hard night's work at trying-out, while Frank was leaning over a water-bucket, rubbing his hands and face with a piece of hard soap, the man at the masthead announced that there was a sail in sight, and in response to the usual inquiry, added: "Broad off the wheather beam. Topsail schooner. Sets low in the water and spreads lots of canvas."

"Do you hear that, Lucas?" cried Frank, gazing about through eyes that were almost hidden in soap suds. "Jump up there, quick!"

The latter cleared his eyes by the aid of a piece of canvas that served him for a towel, and watched the movements of the old boatswain's mate as he hurried aloft. He saw him level his glass, hold it to his eye for a moment and then begin to scramble down again. That was enough for Frank. "Mr. Gale," said he, so delighted and excited. that he could hardly stand still, "my connection with the Tycoon is nearly ended now. My friends are close by."

"I am glad for your sake, sir, and sorry for my own," replied the mate. "We've had a pleasant ship and the best of luck since you've been on the quarter-deck."

"And I have been very well contented," said Frank; "but I wasn't while I was in the forecastle, I tell you. It isn't often that a shanghaied man becomes master of the ship that runs away with him, is it?"

"I never heard the like before, sir."

"And probably you never will again. Well, Lucas!"

"It's the Stranger, sir! I can tell her among a million!" replied the second mate, no less delighted than his captain.

"Breakfast is on, sir," announced the steward.

Frank did not want any, but he made a show of eating nevertheless. He drank a cup or two of a decoction of parched beans which the steward called coffee, swallowed a few mouthfuls of salt horse and hard-tack, and then hurried on deck to tell the officer on watch to see one of the boats clear for lowering, and to have a crew, whom he mentioned by name, ready to pull him off to the schooner. After that he gave his black suit a good overhauling; but it had seen pretty hard service before he drew any clothing from the slop-chest, and he decided that it would not do to put on. Then he took a look at himself in the little mirror that was screwed fast to one of the bulkheads in the cabin, and told himself that Boson was a beauty compared to him.

"Well, what's the difference?" thought Frank. "If any of those boys had been in my boots they would look just as rough and weather-beaten as I do."

With this reflection to console him Frank hurried on deck again, and taking the glass Lucas offered him, levelled it at the schooner, which was now close aboard. Almost the first man he saw was Dick Lewis. Frank's heart leaped at the sight of him. He had supposed that the two trappers were safe in the mountains long before this time, but now he would have a chance to shake them by the hand once more before he bade them good-by for ever. He wondered how they had conquered their fears sufficiently to venture out to sea. He saw Uncle Dick Gaylord and his two officers on the quarter-deck, and the Club gathered in the waist, every one of them with his field-glass in his hand.

"Of course they will recognise the ship, but they will never know me in this dress," thought Frank. "And I don't think they'll be able to make much out of my hail either."

Frank kept out of sight until the ship's main

21

yard was backed and the schooner thrown up into the wind; then he showed himself.

"What ship is that?" yelled a stentorian voice, that Frank could have recognised anywhere.

"The whale ship Eli Coon, Hank Wilson master. Seventeen months out of Nantucket and nine hundred barrels of oil in the hold. I think that bothered them a little, Mr. Gale. I see they are talking very earnestly. Is that crew ready? I'll send a boat aboard of you," he added, hailing the schooner.

"Ay, ay, sir!" answered Uncle Dick, in a tone of voice which indicated that he did not understand the matter at all.

Lucas, Barton, Boson and Tully, all good oarsmen, comprised the boat's crew, and they were not long in taking their captain alongside the schooner. Seeing that the Club and Uncle Dick kept their glasses levelled at him, Frank drew his hat low over his forehead, and thanked the wind for turning the collar of his shirt up around his ears. He laughed to himself when he thought how amazed his friends would be to see him in those clothes and learn that he was the captain of the Tycoon—he who had been shanghaied and thrust into her forecastle to do duty as a common sailor! He thought he could have some sport with the schooner's company, and run no risk of being recognised. After comparing his reckoning with Uncle Dick's, he would slap the boys on the back and take all sorts of liberties with them, and see what they would do about it. But Dick Lewis upset all these calculations in short order. His sharp eyes penetrated Frank's disguise, and no sooner did his head appear above the schooner's rail than he was hauled aboard, lifted bodily from the deck and carried aft. He struggled hard to free himself, but the trapper held him fast, and finally stood him on his feet in front of Uncle Dick, just as he had done with the bogus captain.

"What do you mean?" demanded Frank, in a gruff voice. "If this is the way you treat your visitors, sir, I'll go back where I belong!"

Uncle Dick stared at Frank, who tried to look

angry, but his eyes laughed in spite of himself. "Nelson!" he exclaimed, at a venture.

"That's jest who he are, cap'n," cried the trapper, bringing his heavy hand down on Frank's shoulder with such force that he shook all over. "Whiskers and all, that's him."

It was all out now, and Frank's little plan was exposed. Of course a great hubbub arose at once, and Frank judged by the greeting he received that his friends were just as glad to see him as he was to see them. Lucas and Barton met with an equally cordial reception from their friends in the forecastle, who were not a little surprised to find that one of them had worked his way to the quarter-deck during his absence.

Frank had a long story to tell, and it took him a long time to tell it. When it was ended, Uncle Dick and the Club had a good many questions to ask, and it took a long time to answer them; so that the two vessels remained alongside the greater part of the day. During that time boat's crews were exchanged, some of the schooner's company going off to visit the ship, and some of her crew coming back to visit the Stranger.

As soon as the conversation began to flag Frank spoke of the needs of the wounded captain, asking for some of the good things with which the Stranger was so amply provided; but Uncle Dick had something better to propose. "Write an order to your mate to send him off here," said he. "I have a medicine-chest, plenty of lint and bandages, and long experience has made me a passable physician and surgeon. I can take better care of him than you can, and perhaps he will feel easier when he is out of reach of his men."

Frank was only too glad to accept this kind offer, for he knew that the wounded man would be benefited by the change. He sent off an order to Mr. Gale, and half an hour afterward Captain Barclay was comfortably settled in the Stranger's cabin. He was delighted with his elegant quarters, and repeatedly declared that he did not deserve the treatment he received. If he was ever able to take the quarter-deck again he would be a different man.

His story told and all questions asked and answered, the young captain made ready to return to his ship. Of course all the boys went with him. Frank warned them that he could not give them such food or such quarters as they had on board the Stranger, but they didn't care for that. They wanted to see the Tycoon, and they made Frank promise, over and over again, that if the opportunity were offered, he would show them the operation of catching a whale. The Club tried to induce the trappers to go with them, but their entreaties and arguments fell on deaf ears. Dick and Bob knew that the Stranger was a safe boat, but they did not like to trust the Tycoon, and so thought it best to remain where they were.

"Brace for'ard main yard," said Frank, when all the whaler's boats had been hoisted at the davits. "Eugene, you said you couldn't understand how it came that you reached the Sandwich Islands three days after we did. Now I'll show you. Set studding sails, Mr. Gale."

Eugene very soon found out why it was. The Stranger was considered to be remarkably swift for a small vessel, but the big Tycoon sailed two miles to her one, and at daylight the next morning the schooner was out of sight.

Frank being impatient to reach Honolulu, did not go out of his way to find whales. According to promise he kept the mast-head manned, but to no purpose. The boys watched and waited in the hope of hearing the welcome cry, "There she blows!" but not a whale was to be seen. Mr. Gale told them that the reason was because they offered no inducement. It was the practice of whalers under such circumstances as these, he said, to put up a prize of some kind to go to the man who discovered the first spout. He had known a whale to rise in less than two minutes after a pair of trowsers had been hung up in the rigging.

"O, if that's the trouble, we'll raise so many

that you won't know which to go after first," said
Archie; "who's got any money?"

All the boys happened to have a little in their
pockets, and by clubbing together they raised sufficient to purchase one of the best suits of clothing
in the slop-chest—hat, boots and all—which was
hung up in plain view of the crew. But the offer
of a dozen suits would not have enabled the men to
see whales where there were none, and Frank took
the ship into Honolulu without having the opportunity to gratify his friends, who were greatly dis-
appointed. The Stranger was not in port, but she
came shortly afterward, and by that time the Tycoon's business was settled. She passed through
the consul's hands, the crew were paid off and discharged and a new captain assumed command and
made ready to take her to the States. As soon as
the Stranger came in, Uncle Dick's charge was carried to the hospital, and Frank never heard of him
afterward. He never heard of Mr. Gale either
after he took leave of him. The last time he saw
him he was second mate of the Tycoon.

One incident happened on board the Stranger that is worth recording. It was noticed that after Captain Barclay was brought on board, Dick Lewis acted more like himself than he had done for many a day.

It was observed, too, that he often went through a most expressive pantomime, which was easily understood by those who witnessed it. One morning the captain came out of his cabin and found him standing at the top of the companion ladder, where he had been often seen of late. "Why do you hang around here so much?" asked Uncle Dick.

The trapper pushed his hat on the back of his head, shoved up his sleeves until his brawny arms were bare to the elbow, spread out his feet, placed his hands on his hips and looked at the captain. "When is that mean varmint comin' up?" said he. "I owe him a leetle something, an' I'm in an amazin' hurry to pay it!"

"Now, Lewis, you needn't worry about him," said Uncle Dick. "He's having as much punish-

ment as he can stand. Frank heaped hot coals
of fire on his head every day for three weeks, and
I am following up the same treatment."

"Sho!" exclaimed the trapper, looking doubtfully at Captain Gaylord.

"It is as true as gospel."

Dick could not refuse to believe it after so strong
an affirmation as this. He grinned all over with
delight, and taking the sailor's sturdy palm in his
long, bony fingers, gave it a shake and a squeeze
that made the captain wince and lift one of his feet
a little way from the deck. Then Dick hurried off
to find his chum.

"It's all right, Bob," said he, gleefully. "I
didn't know civilized folks done sich things, but the
cap'n's scalpin' that feller in a way the Injuns
never thought of. He's pilin' fire on his head
every day."

This piece of news, while it greatly surprised both
the trappers, afforded them the liveliest satisfaction.
The kidnapper was being fearfully punished for
what he had done, and they told one another that

he deserved it. Dick did not hang around the cabin door any more, but he kept his eyes open, and as he never saw any fire carried below, he began to grow suspicious.

When the Stranger arrived in the port of Honolulu and he saw preparations being made to take the captain ashore, he resolved to investigate things a little, just to satisfy himself. Watching his chance, while the wounded man was being carried across the deck to be lowered into the boat, he dashed forward and lifted the hat from his head. To his intense surprise and chagrin the captain's scalp was all there, and his hair did not look as if it had ever been near a fire. Knowing nothing of the Christian principle of returning good for evil, the trapper supposed that Captain Gaylord had been piling literal coals on his patient's head every day. It took Uncle Dick a long time to explain things, and the backwoodsman never had as much faith in him after that.

Having restored Frank to the society of his friends once more, we will take leave of him for the present, promising to say more of him soon in the concluding volume of this series, which will be entitled: " THE BOY TRADERS; OR, THE SPORTSMAN'S CLUB AMONG THE BOERS."

THE END.

www.ingramcontent.com/pod-product-compliance
Lightning Source LLC
Chambersburg PA
CBHW031143120726
47905CB00006B/1796